... if you are one of those people who loves to cosy up to a warm fireplace of a cold November's evening, with the rain driving piteously against your windows outside, and you have already read and discovered the dark literary pleasures of *Bram Stoker, M.R. James, Edgar Allan Poe, Algernon Blackwood, Ambrose Bierce, Sheridan Le Fanu*, and many other masters of the macabre - then this book was written for you, enjoy...

"Barry sucks the reader in with a heightened sense of foreboding and unease. His depiction of the surroundings and infernal happenings at the Hellfire Club are cinematic in quality."—**Sunday Independent**

"I have just read The Devil's Hoof by Jonathan Barry. Wow! If you like a Gothic horror story this is the one for you." — **Tom McCaughren**, *Author.*

"Barry writes as well as he illustrates which will be a delight to his many fans. I heartily recommend this book." — **Ronan McGreevy**, *The Irish Times.*

"THE DEVIL'S HOOF"

A Gothic Tale

by
JONATHAN BARRY

Glass Darkly Press
Dublin
2017

Published in 2017 by
Glass Darkly Press, Dublin, Ireland.
Reprinted in August, 2018.
Reprinted in September, 2021.
Reprinted in August, 2022.
Reprinted in January, 2024.

ISBN-13:-978-1-5272-04430

Typeset in 12 on 14.5 point Quadraat
Cover design by POD Digital, Dublin.
Printed in Ireland.

I dedicate this book to three people.

Firstly, to my late lovely father, **John Barry** (1929 – 2015), who gave me a lifetime's passion for literature and music. He taught me the values of kindness, compassion, dignity, and courage.

Secondly, to my beloved late friend, **Brother Declan Murphy** (1930 – 2016), of Mount Mellery Abbey, in Waterford, Ireland, for over forty years of unfailing friendship, consummate wisdom, great laughter, and human understanding.

Finally, to my mother, **Maureen Barry** (who discovered I could draw, write and paint), I owe a lifetime of thanks for her endless creative input, tireless encouragement, and unflinching support.

CONTENTS

I

RAINDROPS IN THE DUST

They say that the Devil has the power to assume a pleasing shape – and if this is so, then I have seen his smiling face. You must not think that I exaggerate when I speak of such things, because, of the horrors which I now recount, I swear by all that is sacred to me, they are true. Of course I realize that in the twilight of one's years it can be easier to soften the distant memories of our past, but I could as soon forget my name, as relinquish the burning images that return to haunt me from the shadows of those restless days. They were real. I was there. And I have survived to tell this tale.

My name is Daniel Parsons, and I must consider myself lucky to have enjoyed a privileged childhood where I grew up in the quiet village of Knutsford, in the county of Cheshire, in my native England. My father had amassed a considerable fortune, most of which he inherited from my grandfather's land speculations in Ireland at the close of the seventeenth century. Of the customs of Ireland I knew precious little, and of its people lesser still, but my father was keen to regale me in my childhood with the countless adventures of my grandparent's struggles to work the celtic landscape for their own gain. He relished the chance to tell me of the wild Irish or ' woodkernes', who my grandfather insisted had still lived in Ireland's forests when he was alive, where they waited in hiding to attack the English invaders. Endless stories of pitched battles between the Irish pike-men and the English cavalry were often the talk of our parlour on many a cold winter's evening.

It would be unfair to suggest that my father recalled these stories as literal facts, as they were frequently told with a nod and a wink, with considerable mirth added in the telling. Neither should it ever be conjectured that he harboured any ill feeling to the natives of that land. He contended to his dying days that the best friend a man could have in all the world, would always be 'a steadfast Irishman, stout of heart, and brave of limb,' a sentiment that made a great impression upon me as a youth. Whether he referred to someone specific from his past, or to Irishmen in general, he never told me.

During my teenage years my father's influence in society had allowed him to secure for me a position of clerk to the local magistrate in Knutsford, a role I worked diligently at until my twenty sixth birthday. I was eager to give a good account of myself and developed during these years a reputation for honesty and a dogged determination to get things done. It was then, in that fateful autumn of 1741, that my father's ambitions for me took a new turn. He had made contact with some of the judiciary in Dublin, (aided no doubt by old family acquaintances who still remembered my grandfather) and pressed for my appointment to a vacancy that had arisen suddenly at the seat of power in Dublin Castle.

I was to be made Secretary to the Prime Sergeant's Office, a position my father said would open many grand opportunities for me. He also maintained that such a situation would make a man of me, and put me in an income of £20 pounds a year – a handsome salary for someone of my age. In truth I felt some anxiety at accepting the offer, and a certain irritation at having to leave my beloved Cheshire, but my father convinced me that the experience would place me in an enviable position to return to England in later years, where I could advance my career to a very senior level.

And so it was that in October of that year, I was posted from England to the Lord Lieutenant's residency in Dublin Castle. I wish my father had warned me more candidly about the vagaries of the Irish climate, because my first two weeks in the capital city had witnessed a veritable assault of cold and damp on my constitution, combined with that feature most associated with Dublin – a deluge of rain that falls at a peculiar angle, which is guaranteed to penetrate the heaviest of all overcoats. I had little or no opportunity to explore the cobbled lanes or fine streets of this venerable old city, but sat shivering at my desk where I familiarised myself with my many duties and the conventions of castle etiquette.

This is how events ran for me during my first few weeks, until, without any warning I was summoned to the Prime Sergeant's Office and was informed that I must postpone my normal duties, to concentrate on the investigation of a series of murders in the village of Glenboyne, a scattered hamlet not twenty miles outside the capital's walls. Twenty miles perhaps, but through wind, rain, mud and mountain it might have been another world – as I would soon discover. My instructions were clear; I was to stamp out these killings, find those responsible, and bring them in chains before the law courts of the King's Bench in Dublin. If reason would not prevail, I was to execute my duties accordingly with any means at my disposal. But at all costs I was to deal with the matter quickly and efficiently. A small guard of soldiers would accompany me, and I could choose any personnel that might assist me in the affair. I had not expected such an onerous task so soon and tried to protest my lack of experience – but to no avail. I was advised that the Viceroy himself was uneasy about the murders and wanted the matter brought to a swift conclusion. My father's zeal had given them their man.

Though the years have gathered round me now, I can still recall with perfect vision that memorable morning when we left the din and smoke of Dublin's city walls. I was excited at the prospect of seeing the Irish landscape I had heard of for so long, but could not keep certain dark thoughts from crowding in on my mind, as to the uncertainty of what lay ahead. We travelled for many hours beyond the perimeter of the city, until, by early evening, we had reached Butterfield, where we changed our horses. Here, with the sun soon waning, I was anxious we should press ahead. All colour, smell and sound from the city was now obliterated far behind us. The wind had got up strongly that evening, and as I watched I saw the late rays of the autumn sun dropping slowly behind a thickening mass of cloud. Below its crimson glow I discerned clearly the strong outline of the Dublin Mountains spreading out on the dull horizon. We continued our journey for several miles, until our route began to climb by slow gradation to the base of the mountain range. At a point in the road, our conveyance approached an unmarked crossroads, and banging on the coach's door I signalled to the driver to rein the horses in, and bring them to a halt.

Craning my head from the open window, I noticed a slight but distinct chill begin to creep upon me, as I watched the pensive soldiers seated atop the transport, their redcoats providing meagre warmth against the keen Irish air. While feeling unsure of which turning to take, through the shadows I perceived the figure of an old man, shuffling slowly towards the intersection ahead of us at the fore of some cattle – a solitary figure in an otherwise desolate landscape. As though anticipating my thoughts the driver pulled the vehicle up to the centre of the junction, to cut across his path and seek direction. It might be our only chance before twilight descended on us.

"You there!" I cried, "Can you help us? Are you familiar with these parts?"

The old man raised his head, and eyed me, and the coach, with deep suspicion. His shrunken face was partly shaded by the dusk of the evening, but even in the grey light I could see that his features seemed somewhat agitated by my question. His hair was a collection of tangled white locks, which fell about his shoulders in great profusion.

"We have just come from Dublin, and are not familiar with these roads. Perhaps you could direct us?" I continued.

Seeming to find courage the listless figure took several steps towards me, until he stood adjacent to the door, where he leaned forward with his face sitting inches from my own. Resting a mottled hand on the open sill, his eyes met mine with a startling gaze, which made me shift uncomfortably in my position. Those pupils seemed to roam all over me with a wildness I did not understand, before mumbling through the side of his mouth –

"Oh yes, Sir, indeed for sure, Sir," – sniffling as he spoke – "I know these lands hereabouts, having worked them close on forty years, Sir. But I see you are on the King's business?" – this last comment made as he glanced at the coronet on the polished door.

"Why there's not been a coach this way for near on three weeks, Sir! And you surely won't be travelling far on a night like this?"

"On a night like this? What do you mean?" I retorted.

"Why I've been watching the sky since noontime, Sir, and that cloud can only mean but one thing – a storm – and a terrible one at that, which I hope to shelter from before darkness settles in."

In so saying, he motioned with his head towards the anvil-shaped cloud, which even as he gestured, towered ominously on the horizon, its truculent bulk stretching ever higher into the darkening sky. It had until now escaped my notice, but as if in answer to the old man's warning small but steady drops began to stain the dusty earth about his feet.

"Yes, of course... of course, you are probably right. But our business is pressing, and we cannot lose any time. We are looking for the village of Glenboyne. Are we on the right road?" I persisted.

Then something happened that I could not forget where I to live for a thousand years. The old man's face turned an ashen grey as he fixed me with a look of abject terror. It was like the dread of a condemned man who walks his last journey to the foot of the gallows. His muscles tightened in an instant, and a sickly pallor crossed his face, as though his arteries were drained of blood before my very eyes. He wrenched his hand from the door and fell backwards in a paroxysm of fear. What manner of behaviour was this, I thought? Was the old fellow mad? What could have disturbed him so much? Perhaps a sickness had come upon him in this chill wind? The latter seemed most likely, but while I grappled with my thoughts, he had already beaten a hasty retreat from the vehicle's side.

"For God's sake man! What is wrong? No – don't go. Where is Glenboyne? Wait! At least point us in the right direction!"

The aged figure shook his head in violent refusal, but seeing my intention to dismount, he waved his arms reluctantly towards the road along which he had just come. To my great perplexity he also made the Sign of the Cross above his chest, before muttering in a broken voice –

"May God have mercy on your souls!"

"Straight ahead then?" I called after him. "But wait! What about...?"

"I think we should be moving on, Mr. Parsons," came a second voice from within the coach.

I motioned to speak again, but the frail form had already vanished down the road with a speed that belied his age, where it seems he found his cattle, that had long since passed him, delighted at the chance to dally on the roadside.

"Harkin! It must be the road in front. Move on!"

"Yes, Mr. Parsons! Straight ahead, Sir," replied the coachman.

Straining at the bit the horses shook their manes, and in an instant the conveyance shot away, the wheels churning up the earth in a cloud of broken dust. The rattle of the hoops, the creak of the axles, and the thumping of the hooves shattered the silence as we hurtled towards the road. The track was featureless except for a line of grass and weeds, which marked out the centre of its course across the open bog.

"May God have mercy on your souls!" The old man's words were still ringing in my ears. What did he mean, and what was he afraid of?

II

A MISSHAPEN FORM

With uneasy thoughts I threw my head back against the leather rail, desirous to find a comfortable position, but a sudden jolt from the wheels demonstrated the folly of such a notion. Instead I sat upright and addressed my sole companion, who had spoken but a moment earlier.

"Well, Father, it would appear we are moving in the right direction. We should at least reach Kelly's Gorge by nightfall, I suppose? And Glenboyne village, you told me earlier, is but a mile beyond this valley – did you say?"

The cleric turned his gaze from the darkening landscape, and shifting forward into the lamplight, he showed his figure plainly. In attire he was dressed from head to toe entirely in black, and while his long cloak and deep hood often hid his form, it revealed enough to show he was a man of strong build and broad shoulders. His short black hair was thick set, and although greying around his temples it was not unkempt. Of his age I suspected he had passed his fortieth year, but he spoke in a tone and manner of a much younger man. He had a rough but kindly face, and his hazel eyes twinkled both with intelligence and an inner wisdom. Above all, it was his laugh that I remember most – a deep hearty boom, that travelled loud and far, lifting the spirits of those that were lucky enough to hear it.

I had known Fr. Declan Moynihan less than a week, but already I regarded him with a genuine respect. He was a monk of the Benedictine Order of the Abbey of St. John, and I knew that he had studied the occult for several years on the continent, where he had gained a considerable reputation. I was also aware that as a priest he had been forced to flee Ireland under the Penal Laws, but a recent slight relaxing of the law had allowed him to return to his native soil, where he had to register at Dublin Castle under strict regulation.

Most importantly of all, I had been informed that as a young cleric he had spent some time in the parish of Glenboyne, and that his knowledge of both the area and its people might prove invaluable to me. My orders were to grant him greater freedom of practice, should he aid me in solving these crimes. I personally felt that to use him in this way was wrong, but I had no say in the matter.

"We'll reach Glenboyne alright. Have no fear of it, boy," replied the black figure in a soft Cork accent. "It's been many years since I was last here, and the roads were more familiar to me then. But I feel sure we will recognise certain landmarks as we progress along our way."

As he spoke I noticed through the satin curtains that the landscape had altered considerably. Our transport had gained the summit of a grassy knoll, and rounding a spur in the road, we opened out into a rocky grove. Here the path showed increasing signs of neglect, where great swathes of ferns and sprawling brambles threatened the roadside. Many ferns lay crushed and rotten, where frequent rain and the yellowing of autumn had taken their toll. On either side the mountains now towered black against the sky, sloping down steeply in great fastnesses of rock. I listened as a deep rush of wind, which started somewhere high above, now moved phantom-like down the side of the craggy ravine. Suddenly, a sheet of hailstones burst from the firmament and lashed the coach with ferocious volume, and as it did, I heard the soldiers cursing up above, shifting on their benches, their great surtouts flapping occasionally across my view.

"Father, what do you know about the murders?" I asked directly.

"As little as you have told me, Mr. Parsons," he replied somewhat tersely.

"I think I would prefer it if you called me Daniel from now on, Father."

"Well then – as little as you have told me, Daniel," he repeated.

Leaning forward I reached into a satchel beside my feet.

Its blackened leather hide had seen brighter days, but it travelled wherever I did, and rarely left my side. Groping for some moments I produced a newspaper, creased and slightly torn, and handed it to him.

It was a small enough article, but holding it to the lamplight, the monk began to read: "... BRUTAL MURDER OF TWO WOMEN... It has been recorded by the Justice of the Peace, for the Barony of Upper Cross in the Dublin Mountains, that in the village of Glenboyne, two violent deaths have occurred within a fortnight, of two women. While a full report has not yet been received from the local burgess, it is understood that both were viciously attacked, with lacerations to their entire bodies and faces. The reason for these assaults is uncertain – perhaps they were the grim result of thefts that went horribly wrong? But they are another example of the lawlessness that threatens the decent men and women of this nation, and on behalf of our readers, The Dublin Weekly Journal would appeal to the King's Bench to enforce the law, and bring these criminals to swift justice..."

Lowering the paper the priest thought for a moment.

"This would seem to be suggesting that a frustrated robbery in which the ruffians did not get their reward ended in savage slaughter?" he remarked.

"Do you think this likely?" I ventured.

"Well, theft is certainly common," he replied, "and

the times are desperate enough for anything. These last two winters have left the people starving and wretched, Daniel – famine has left their fields untilled and yielding nothing. They would kill a man for less than an oatcake if they got a chance. I heard of a poor soul on Thomas Street beaten half to death, and stripped of his cloak, his waistcoat, and his breeches. They even took his silk stockings! And this in the laneway behind the rectory!"

Here he broke off briefly with a loud laugh, but checking himself he resumed his serious demeanour.

"And yet, I sense there is something more at work here, a bloody hand with a deeper motive."

Then raising his eyes to address me, he said drily – "You would not have instructed me to come with you, had you not suspected so yourself?"

Catching his steady gaze, a wry and knowing smile crept across my face, and with a little embarrassment that admitted no loss of pride, I dropped my head in acknowledgment of the truth. I continued however to press him further.

"Father! What do you know of Jack Buckley and the Hellfire Club?"

A gust of wind rocked against the casement as I spoke these words, and the priest rose suddenly, turning on me with a withering and fearsome expression.

"Those unholy names should not be uttered lightly, young man, if uttered by any at all!"

He stood above me for several moments wavering, agitated it seemed to me by some inner turmoil. Regaining his seat he continued more calmly.

"So, you have heard of The Hellfire Club? I should have guessed. I know little about Jack Buckley, but it is true that many years ago I met briefly with his father, Sir Richard Buckley. He owned all these lands from Three Rock Mountain, to Featherbed Bog, including the village of Glenboyne. Sir Richard was a wicked old soul, much given over to gaming and vice. It was said that he had set up the club as a kind of secret society for brazen young dandies and wayward delinquents. That is all I know. But do not ask me to speak more on these matters. Some memories should be left alone and in the dark. There will be another time and place for us to discuss this subject, but it is not tonight."

He had aroused my curiosity, but as I pondered his words, a bolt of lightning, white and brilliant, rent the sky, illuminating the coach in spectacular fashion. A second flash, this time brighter and closer than the first, ripped across the trees, revealing in its wake a panoramic splendour of mighty slopes and pointed crags. It was then that I saw it, standing at the head of the valley – a rock formation, striking to behold.

"Father! Look! On the summit. What is it?"

Grabbing his arm and lowering the window, we thrust our heads into the elements to view the strange structure. The hail had now given way to icy rain, and only for an instant did a further flash from the heavens reveal its shape. It was a mighty slab, set above three triangular stones, and shining brightly on the mountaintop. It stood perched above the precipitous mass of two granite escarpments, which seemed to form a natural barrier, as if guarding the entrance to some secret realm. The soldiers had also spotted it and were loudly shouting to each other. Then, all too quickly, like a fabulous apparition, it was lost to sight. Still gripping his arm I turned to the cleric hopeful for an explanation.

"The Giant's Grave," he said in a hushed tone, "it's an ancient cairn that marks the entrance to Kelly's Gorge," and as he spoke these words, I saw him grasp something close to his chest. It was a small bone crucifix that hung like a talisman around his neck. Before I could examine it further, a blast of chilling rain drove us back from the window's ledge. A low and sonorous boom then followed, as the thunder, muffled at first and rumbling in the distance, now broke powerfully above the treetops.

The jolted horses, maddened by the effect, redoubled their speed with violent energy, and plunged headlong through the entrance of the gorge. To my surprise we entered into a ravine of wild undergrowth and mature woodland. Great throngs of copper beech rose high into the air, their grey trunks shimmering in the dismal light. After what seemed an interminable age, the gallery of trees fell away to reveal a sharp precipice, down which the track twisted in torturous curves. Descending further still, it became a muddy trough as torrents of water poured freely along its verges. Cloud and sky were now impossible to tell apart, and through the pall of filthy rain I wondered how the driver could possibly hold his course.

Then without any warning, I felt the coach pull dangerously to one side, and as if thrust by its own momentum, it slid helplessly out of control, before grinding to a halt. Half angry at the coachman's carelessness, but thankful we had not crashed, I flung the door open to determine the cause of his abrupt action.

We had entered a dense overgrown hollow.

"Harkin! Have you lost your head?"

But the driver was still confused, and before he could answer I saw a sight that chilled me to the bone. In the mire, a dozen feet to the right of where we swerved, I saw another vehicle – a chaise, lying on its side in the middle of the road, its wheels still turning in the driving rain. Around its frame a flood of water several inches deep spilled across its path, where a stream appeared to have burst its banks, and was now issuing forth onto the roadside. Worse still, a flicker of lightning showed a body lying near the chaise, its limp and lifeless form splayed out on the ground. Even as I watched I could see that the level of the water was rising as the storm intensified.

While I stood transfixed, the solid bulk of Fr. Moynihan bounded past me to where the stricken vehicle had fallen on its side. I followed fast on his heels until I reached his crouching figure. There before us was the body of a man, lying on his back amongst a flotsam of clothes and splintered wood. A gash upon his forehead displayed a grievous wound, and not far from where he lay, beyond the road's edge, a trail of blood and track marks showed evidence of some struggle. Leaning forward on one knee the monk raised the head of the inanimate person, and as he did so, it seemed to me that a certain object caught his eye, which he fingered in the mud.

He turned his head sharply towards me, and I saw in his eyes a look of trepidation.

"This man is still alive. Hurry, Daniel, and help me with him. We must get out of here at once."

I roused myself to action and turned to address the soldiers.

"You lot! Get down here. Watch the trees and if you see anything that moves – shoot it. Harkin! Hop down and examine the wheels and check the horses. Now move – quickly – all of you."

The cluster of redcoats tumbled down off the rooftop

and took up different positions on the road. The storm threw out its anger as furious gusts rose and swelled, buffeting the treetops with brutal ferocity. The voice of the priest beckoned to me.

"Help me get him into the coach. He is badly hurt, but I think he can make it. Get your shoulder under his arm."

Both of us struggled in the mud to raise the body from the ground, and as we did so the stranger's eyes parted slightly, as he regained consciousness for a brief moment. His deathly colour revealed his weakened state, and rolling his head, he choked to tell us something. In a rasping voice he finally spoke.

"My little baby... my Nan. It's got my Nan," he gasped.

A rattling sound began in his throat, and as his head slumped forward onto his chest, his words became inaudible. Dragging his feet through the sludge, we continued to haul the bulky weight of the man, until both of us collapsed with him through the coach door.

A piercing blast shot through the air, as something whistled through the trees.

Turning swiftly, I saw the outline of one of the soldiers standing close to a grove of trees, where he had discharged his firelock.

"What was it?" I cried. "Did you see something?"

"Over there, Sir! I'm not sure!"

I directed my eyes to a canopy of foliage set in off the track, where here or there, great shapes disclosed themselves as broken tree-trunks or sloping boulders. But something else was there also, blacker than the night and deep within the thicket – a misshapen form, large, rigid, and silent. I felt my hands tremble as an unknown fear began to grip me.

"One of the wheels is jammed, Mr. Parsons – stuck solid behind a rock."

The wretched face of Harkin shone frantically at me through the rain.

"What? Are you sure? Can we dig it out with our hands?"

"No, Sir! But with enough shoulders and elbow grease we should be able to push her up and over it."

"Then let's do it. I'm sorry, Father, but I'll need your help also."

The priest was already on his feet, and calling on the other soldiers, I instructed them to join him.

A second shot rang out through the darkness. The private who had fired off his musket had now entered the grove and was no longer visible. A turbulent motion of wind-tossed leaves and thrashing branches was all that could be seen. Then from the tapestry of shadows an agonised scream from the soldier called out – his piteous cries striking terror in our veins.

Seizing my pistol from the coach I ran to where I had last seen him, but the rising water kept me back. Then from the trees a peculiar sound began, a malevolent hissing noise like a giant snake spitting in its lair. A thud of crunching twigs grew closer, and the hissing now changed into a harrowing roar. Growing stronger still, its dreadful cry convulsed the air with appalling and unnatural volume.

Raising my weapon, and cocking back the hammer, I groped furiously for my powder keg, which hung from my neck on a leather strap. Fumbling in the darkness my grimy fingers seized the small ivory container. Each second seemed a lifespan as I struggled to unhasp the stubborn peg that kept the powder dry. Another roar, more terrible than the first, caused me to stumble, and slipping from my grasp, the keg escaped its strap and tumbled headlong into the pummelling water. Biting my lip I threw myself to the ground, and thrusting out my hand to grasp the floating object, I watched in horror as it slid beyond my reach and further down into the swollen brook. Without the keg my pistol was useless, and seized with panic I fled back to the others and rejoined their effort.

"Push! As hard as you can, all together... PUSH!" Our nervous hands gripped tight the under-rail as we pressed our shoulders to the rear of the conveyance. With clenched teeth we arched our backs and heaved with all our strength. The chassis creaked and for a moment rose above the mud, where it tottered briefly, before slumping back behind the stubborn rock. As he whipped the horses mercilessly I heard Harkin urging them on. With resumed energy we pushed once more, the wooden hulk creaking under the pressure. Lifting slowly, the muddied spokes scaled the obstacle, and with one last effort the horses darted forward, wrenching the wheel from the furrow. The abruptness of the motion caught me unaware, and I stumbled forward, striking downwords against the chassis. In the confusion I collapsed to the ground.

Before I knew it, a flurry of many hands plucked me from the mud, and with an extraordinary strength, (begotten no doubt by the terror of the moment), I felt them haul me onto the safety of the coach floor. The vehicle sped away as the frenzied horses broke across the brook, cutting through the water with the keenness of a knife. The unspeakable howl was heard once more, but it faded in the wind as the hollow fell further behind us. As I slouched on the floor, I saw Fr. Moynihan clasping the bone crucifix around his neck, while with shut eyes he offered up a silent prayer. Then all turned to darkness and I remembered nothing more.

III

THE EAGLE TAVERN

As I opened my eyes a series of blurred shadows crossed my view. Blinking several times, my focus slowly returned to reveal that I was lying on my back staring at a thatched roof supported by black oaken beams. I moved to stir myself, when the welcome features of Fr. Moynihan leant forward to greet me. With a relieved smile he said –

"Well now, boy! Aren't you the lucky one to be alive? You got yourself a couple of nice-looking bruises there – but sure – you're well able for it!"

I forced myself into a sitting posture, and as I did so a stinging pain rose with me to the top of my head, and I felt a dull ache spread across my torso. I clasped my forehead to encounter a small swelling which hurt to the touch, and looking down I saw a purple wound across my chest, which had obviously been bleeding. I noticed in the shadows Corporal Wilkinson standing guard near the door, leaning on his musket. On seeing his redcoat, the horrors of our recent adventure broke suddenly back upon my mind.

"Sweet God! What happened at the hollow, Father? That man we found! Who was he? Did he make it alive?"

I sat up on the side of the bed, a little unsure of my balance.

"Where are we? Did we make it to Glenboyne? And what about that soldier? I heard his screams. Did anyone go back to find him? What in God's name got him?"

My arm shook slightly in my agitation, as the monk responded.

"We have reached Glenboyne and are safe and sound at the hospitality of The Eagle Tavern. I'm afraid you have been asleep a full day and night, but mercifully the landlord's daughter has been quite thorough in treating your wounds. You fell down sharply on one of the axles, and it is a miracle it did not cut through your chest too deeply." He paused here briefly.

"She has been bathing it since you arrived, and thanks to her dressings the bleeding has stopped, and the swelling is all but gone. As regards that man— well... " – the priest's gaze glanced at the floor.

"I'm afraid he died of his injuries, about six hours ago. All I could gather was that his name was Geoffrey Harold and that he owned a large farm on the outskirts of the village. Whatever killed him also took his daughter Nan. She has disappeared. Wilkinson here returned to the Gorge to search for Private Taylor and the young lady, but could not find either of them."

"Dear God!" I moaned, "another three deaths."

"But surely the girl and Taylor may still be alive?" conjectured the priest.

This comment gave me some hope.

"Very true, Father, and we must act fast. Where are my clothes?"

"But, Daniel, you have barely recovered your strength. Give yourself a few more hours."

"We have no time, Father. If they are still alive, we need to find them quickly. Now Wilkinson – describe to me what you found at the hollow. Was there any sign of these missing persons? You must tell me everything!"

As I wriggled into my shirt, the soldier moved close to the centre of the room, removing his tricorne hat, and fingering it nervously. His face rose to meet mine with a perturbed look upon his brow.

"Well, Mr. Parsons, Sir, while you was recovering I went back to Kelly's Gorge this morning with a small contingent of men in Harkin's coach, and found that same chaise still on its side. We looked everywhere for them, Sir, but we couldn't find a thing, at least – not at first. But then Private Saunders – one of my best men, Mr. Parsons – he noticed on a bank above the road that the branches had been broken back – almost like a bear or something had smashed straight through them! We clambered up, and... " his voice faltered.

"Go on."

"We clambered up and found a fragment of Private Taylor's jacket, Sir, clinging to a branch. It were torn and bloody. Of the girl there was not a trace. Private Saunders entered the thicket first, and spotted a trail where something had been dragged. We followed it as best we could, but the mud and rain had washed much of it away. Until I found a dry patch under a clump of trees... " He paused again.

"Well?" I pursued. I watched his face as he attempted to speak, and saw his features fill with dread.

"What did you see, Wilkinson?"

"Hoof marks, Sir!" His eyes shot a glance at me like a bullet.

"Hoof marks?" I repeated back, "and what is so remarkable in that? At least we know the attackers were on horseback."

"These were no ordinary hoof marks, Sir, and no horse could have made them, unless it walked on its hind legs. They were bigger than any I have ever seen, and I could swear it was a two legged set of prints, not four."

I looked at him in astonishment as I grappled with the implication.

"If not a horse, what else then? My colleagues at Dublin Castle tell me that the Wicklow and Dublin Mountains are brimful of stag. Perhaps this is what you saw – the remains of an illegal stag hunt. Maybe too a rearing horse could have made those marks. Especially in flight. Isn't that so, Father?"

Either because he had no other explanation to offer, or because he did not wish to alarm the Corporal further – the robed figure rallied to my support with something of a feigned air, masking I felt, his own deep unease.

"Yes – yes that is quite possible. Stag are often hunted in the mountains, and they certainly leave heavy tracks. We could be dealing with a band of murderous poachers or highwaymen, who while still hiding in the thickets were caught in the act by Taylor, and not wishing to be discovered they may have knocked him unconscious, and left him somewhere in the woods. Geoffrey Harold's daughter may have suffered a similar fate."

Wilkinson seemed ready to refute this, but a light tap at the door disrupted our conversation. The redcoat raised his musket and motioned to the entrance.

"Come in!" urged Fr. Moynihan.

The iron latch lifted as the door opened sluggishly, while a delicate white hand showed itself to our view. From behind the beams a frightened but beautiful face emerged into the room. She could scarcely have been nineteen years old, maybe less, and her blond ringlets dangled tenderly about her neck. Her fine figure was emphasised by a fitted bodice at the waist, which was hidden under a plain linen apron. The fearful thing blushed and retreated at the sight of the firearm.

"Cathy, child, there is nothing to be afraid of – come in," spoke the churchman.

"I beg your pardon, Father, but you did say to call when I had some food prepared. It is ready now, should you and the gentleman be free to dine."

"Thank you, Cathy. We would be glad to have it. This is Mr. Parsons."

She curtsied and peered shyly at me.

"Thank you for your aid, Miss Cathy," I ventured, "it was most kind of you to attend my wounds – I am very grateful to you."

"You are welcome, Sir. But now, my father is impatient for my return. This way please."

We all rose to follow her, as she slipped out into the corridor. Before I left the room the cleric pulled me by the sleeve, and pressed this warning to my ear.

"Have a care, Daniel," he whispered, "and mind what you say. We will find few friends here, and may not recognise them at first."

We entered a hallway cluttered with barrels, straw, and broken plaster. It had escaped my notice until then that despite the daylight that still issued from outside, the interior of the building was dark and murky, which explained why the girl paused to light a candle with her narrow rushlight. A turn in the passage led us past several empty rooms, their doors ajar, until we reached a cloth covering at the side entrance to a lounge. She dipped under it, and we followed her into a murmur of voices and the smell of corked ale.

The tavern was dimly lit and a pall of yellow smoke seemed to hang from its rafters. From a central beam there hung a single iron chandelier, where broken candles cast more shadow than light on the seated faces. One end of the room was piled with sacks of barley, while the other formed a storehouse of casks and woven baskets. A bar of sorts ran counter to the wall, and two black doors marked the entrance to the street. It was a damp and miserable-looking place, with frame and form being hard to distinguish. Nestling on the floor stood half a dozen tables with rough hewn benches, where several figures sat huddled and motionless. A deathly stillness greeted our entrance, and a host of eyes burnt holes through our flesh. The only cheer was a roaring hearth, where an iron pot and some broken stools framed its healthy glow.

The landlord's daughter motioned us to a small table set back in an alcove, where she laid out a simple fare of baked potatoes, cabbage, and a platter of oatcakes. I had forgotten my hunger and for some moments I demolished every scrap and crumb as if it were a veritable feast. A flagon of ale aided my digestion, and I sighed with relief at this welcome repast. My hooded companion observed my very public satisfaction, but enjoyed his meal in a more subdued fashion.

"Cathy! What are you doing there? Get over here."

This loud command issued from a stout burly fellow, who made with all speed in the direction of our table. His florid complexion and course leather apron left little doubt that he was the proprietor of the tavern. He planted himself firmly in front of us, while his daughter retreated to the safety of the bar. I fancied that a close examination of his face showed a striking resemblance to a leg of boiled mutton, and while I might have laughed aloud under other circumstances, this joint of meat meant serious business.

Ignoring my presence he addressed the priest.

"I'm afraid, Father, we have no rooms for tonight. All are taken."

"How odd?" I interjected, "we just passed a hallway of empty rooms." I stared up at him.

"What is your name landlord?"

The leg of mutton grew irritated, and swelled up to even greater proportions.

"Harry Maguire," he coughed, "and you must be, er,... Mr. Parsons. Yes, well... I am glad you are feeling better, Sir, but you must be on your way."

"I'm afraid that is not possible, Mr. Maguire, and we will be in need of your lodgings until our business here is finished – including the soldiers."

"But you can't! I insist that... "

"I am here on the King's business to investigate a series of recent murders, and until I find the perpetrators of these crimes this establishment will remain our base. We are here to protect you, so you need not be alarmed."

But his obvious indignation now changed to fearful trembling, and desirous not to be overheard he lent forward into my face.

"You don't understand," he croaked, "it's not safe here, not for me, not for my daughter. Please – we want no part in it."

I produced a half crown from my pocket and placed it in his hand.

"You will be sufficiently paid for your time and service, and I'll see to it that a guard is posted at the inn door."

His face twitched a little as his fist closed on the coin. He crouched down even closer.

"Look, Mr. Parsons, - I mean you no offence, but many in this village would say that the black monk and redcoats will only bring more trouble."

I pulled out two guineas and cast them onto the table. His grasping fingers caught them with surprising alacrity.

"I'll see what I can do," he murmured.

"And I'll want some information."

"Of a particular nature?" he wheezed.

"Of a most particular nature."

"I'll try," he whispered, "if the right moment presents itself."

He then rose and performed a perfect pantomime of genial hospitality, wiping the table with a good deal of bluster, and filling our tankards with fresh ale. It was a marvellous display, and one that I felt certain was designed for the benefit of other eyes and ears lurking close by.

"You waste no time, that's for sure," observed the monk. I turned to address him, but before I could utter another word, a clamourous commotion drew our attention to the entrance of the inn. Wild voices and the thread of running boots approached from outside. In an instant the doors were flung apart, and a frantic young man collapsed on his knees, gasping for breath. Several ragged children stood panting behind him, their faces glowing with the pain of their exertions. Quicker than a cat the landlord's daughter ran to his side, and clasped his head in her tender hands.

"Sean! What is it love?"

He lifted his face in obvious turmoil, his eyes welling as he struggled to speak.

"The children found her!" he gasped, "poor sweet Nan! Down by the tombs in the old churchyard. Dead, Cathy – torn to pieces and hanging from a tree!"

His voice broke down in convulsive emotion.

I sprang to my feet with Fr. Moynihan by my side, and advanced with speed to the stricken form.

"Wilkinson!" I shouted, "gather your men as fast as you can."

IV

A GOOD DEAL OF MISCHIEF

"You must take us there at once! Have you got the strength to do it? We will need your help to find her!"

I turned as I addressed these words to the prostrate youth, who rose to gather himself. As he straightened he showed a rugged countenance and athletic figure, and while a certain boorishness marked his bearing, there was no doubting his appearance was a handsome one with a pride to match his features. He wore brown flaxen trousers well worn and frayed near the feet, with a tired white shirt under a rough jacket, and I estimated he was certainly no wiser than his twenty-second year, or a little younger.. He had tousled fair hair tied back at the neck, and staunch blue eyes.

"Dear God, no!" he gasped, his voice tremulous with emotion.

"It is not safe – surely you must know this? There is something out there. Don't you understand? Tell him Cathy! Tell him! Even that old fool McIntyre won't open the turnpike gate – he is terrified to let anyone or anything in or out of the village. He swears he heard and saw something just last night beyond the gate, but what it was he could not say.

I've never seen the old dolt so shook up before."

He directed this outburst to the graceful figure of Cathy Maguire, who tried to support and comfort him.

"You must do as the English gentleman says, Sean. He has come from Dublin to help us, and you must hurry and show him where she is. It will be all right. I will come with you."

Her words had a remarkable effect upon his nerves, as he transposed his fixed gaze from hers to mine, with the words, "I will go then."

I was conscious at the same moment of his utterance that two indistinct figures had passed almost unseen behind me and out through the tavern doors. I was too late to identify their shadowy forms before they had slipped out onto the street. The inn was now alive with hasty whispers and a chorus of exclamations from hitherto unnoticed individuals, who had already been seated in reclusive corners of the building. Like frightened mice issuing forth from every corner of a barn, their peering faces began to emerge into the shimmering firelight, aghast and trembling at what they had heard. Wilkinson returned with several foot soldiers, explaining that while the coach had been able to return to Kelly's Gorge that morning to search the hollow, on its return to the village the axles had given way, and consequently Harkin had left the vehicle with the local blacksmith to repair and strengthen the damaged chassis. We would have to walk the distance, which admittedly made me quite nervous. Minutes later we found ourselves in earnest procession along Glenboyne's charmless thoroughfare, following in Sean's footsteps.

Although evening was now advancing there was plenty of daylight left for me to view the village's principal features. The main street consisted of a worn muddy expanse, with great oaken beams sunk deep into the ground forming an avenue of wooden planks, where horse and cart performed their daily routines. I had seen these oaken streets in Dublin also, but in the capital they had been built with great craft and precision. Here in Glenboyne, the wooden joists were less skilfully placed, with gaps forming along some of the rafters, where a hapless coachman might find his wheel snagged or his mare rendered lame.

On either side of this way there was a row of dismal cabins or huts (a form of cottage designed by the Irish, which my father had described to me in many of his frequent reflections). These huts, or ' cots' as they were more commonly known, consisted of a humble mud cabin made of hardened clay and straw, white-washed on the exterior, with a thatched straw roof to keep out the elements. They had no chimneys, but just a hole in the centre of the structure, which from a distance gave the peculiar visual effect that the building was on fire. Outside these habitations poorly swine and poultry roamed at ease, or slept on scattered straw. Most cabins had small garden plots containing great turf stacks which were piled assiduously on one side of the building to provide fuel for their ever hungry fires. The pungent smell of this burning turf was almost overpowering, but I found its earthy sweetness strangely attractive.

The overall impression upon my mind was of a cheerless spectacle, and the obvious privation of the dwellings seemed to heighten the sense of pervasive gloom. An absence of stone buildings was most marked, but here and there I espied an occasional granite structure or wall. Most notable amongst these was the noble ruin of a Norman tower just beyond the village; its giant battlements silhouetted against the hamlet's skyline. The ages of neglect revealed large holes in its masonry, where a profusion of ivy and the chatter of crows now held sway over all. Its lonely edifice and blackened stones saddened me somehow, as I tried to imagine its walls filled with the noise and industry of centuries past.

All of this I gathered in a few moments from rapid observation, mindful of the heinous task that lay before us. Fr. Moynihan strode vigorously beside me with Sean and Cathy close by his shoulder. Wilkinson had deployed several redcoats on either side of the street, forming a sweeping perimeter ahead of our party. This had the desired effect of discouraging prying eyes, hidden behind the silent doors that we passed, from getting too close to our business. Each of these dwellings seemed to exude a sense of inveterate hate. Occasionally a shoeless child would run out to greet us only to be seized furiously by its mother and dragged back inside, where bolt and latch were fastened. The only company desirous to keep up with us were a band of wild half-starved dogs, many of which roamed in packs along the streets and laneways. They kept up a perfect cacophony of yelps and howls piercing to my ears, and it was with great restraint that I had to stop myself from kicking out at them. Behind us I noticed several onlookers from the Eagle Tavern following in our path, but always keeping a cautious distance.

After several minutes the main street curved left, and following a dip in the incline, it led us past a finely proportioned chapel of superior granite. Its imposing clock tower shimmered in the evening sun and it was encompassed around by a low wall of black iron railings. Nestling on the church's grounds, a rectory of similar design and quality convinced me that this was the home of Glenboyne's resident parson. As we passed this structure I felt conscious of Fr. Moynihan's presence and wondered if he found the building an affront to his beliefs? I pondered too whether he was resentful at being summoned to assist me under duress? This could prove problematic if he decided secretly not to co-operate fully in the investigation. After all, it would be understandable if he felt that way, and I did not want this experience to be unnecessarily difficult or uncomfortable for either of us. To this end I was keen from the start to gain both his trust and respect. But a glance at his face showed that his mind was focused on the turnpike gate that now loomed into view, and turning quickly he pressed his hand against my arm before saying –

"We must keep the barrier open, Daniel, until we locate and retrieve her body. The gatekeeper will be desperate to lock the doors behind us once we pass out, but you must insist he keep them unfastened. Perhaps a soldier posted at the toll-house would suit this purpose? We do not know the strength or number of our foe yet, and must take every precaution."

"It will be arranged, Father," I confirmed.

"There is a ruined monastery not far beyond the turnpike gate, with an ancient cemetery near the roadside," he continued. "It is an old Catholic burial ground where the poor and dispossessed are laid to rest, and it is most likely that this is the place where the children saw her corpse. Whatever we see there it is essential to maintain calm, and that you allow me time to examine her remains. May I suggest you commandeer a wagon from the gatekeeper as it will be necessary to transport her body for decent christian burial."

I admired the cleric's presence of mind, for I had indeed not thought of such practicalities and immediately I sent one of the infantrymen to fetch a cart. As we approached the wooden hulk of the toll-house, Sean ran ahead of us, and ascending the stairs he proceeded to hammer energetically at the door.

"McIntyre! Are you there? We need you to open the gates! Can you hear me? This is an emergency!"

His challenge was answered by a rattling of keys and the sound of a latticed window being unhasped from above. Appearing from the opening a querulous red face slowly emerged, displaying a mixed expression of terror and peevishness. Great lines of apprehension formed on his puckered brow, and such was his irritation that both inflated cheeks seemed ready to explode like two great bellows. His lips were remarkably thin, to the point that where they were pulled back across the gums, his mouth resembled a gash in a slit orange.

"Who is it? Identify yourself!" he thundered.

"It is I – Sean, Sean Matthews," came the reply.

"For heaven's sake, young Matthews, what are you doing here? Get off home lad! You half startled me to death! Who are these people? What is their business?"

I stepped forward into his view, with Wilkinson poised at my side.

"Get a move on!" I urged. "We are here on the authority of the King's Bench to hunt down the killers of Nan Harold and the other unfortunates of this district. My orders are direct from the Prime Sergeant himself and you would be wise to co-operate. Any obstructions will be dealt with seriously by the Justices of the Peace. Now open the turnpike immediately and keep it unbolted until we return. Hurry man!"

"Redcoats be damned," he snapped, "that's no way to speak to the gatekeeper! Of all the nerve! And what will the Reverend Hearne have to say? It is his toll-gate you know, and he will want his fee for passing. Now let's see – how many of you are there? Over half a dozen by the looks of things. Of course if the dogs are with you that will cost more. I'll be generous and charge you the same price as a drove of cattle – you can't get fairer than that – that will be ten pence gentlemen."

The preposterous nature of his comments goaded me to anger, and sensing my impatience Wilkinson advanced up the worn wooden steps with his musket pointed at the window.

"You heard what Mr. Parsons said. Now open those gates double-quick, or by God you'll answer to me. Shift yourself fast!"

Looking down the barrel of a gun seemed to produce a favourable outcome, as the slit orange retreated into the shadows of the toll-house, cursing and spitting, where he proceeded to turn the axle of the gate mechanism. The sounds of the cogs and pulleys groaning soon gave way to the heavy creaking of the wooden doors. Inch by inch the gates parted, and first through the opening was the gang of unruly dogs, exhilarated into action by a sense of adventure. They sprinted up the road like a hunting pack, as if driven on by some scent they had detected on the wind. We followed hard in their direction and made steady progress up the muddied highway. For the briefest of moments the sun broke through the twilight and cast its rays on a rich and varied landscape. Dense woodland dominated the roadsides of a broad valley, where alder, birch, and stately elms shrouded the way with blankets of fallen leaves. Bordering these trees thickets of gorse and heather added their own resplendent colours, some clinging to the glittering display of silver granite boulders that formed a chain around their base. The substantial size and density of these stones caused me to speculate that they must have been the remnants of a large rock-fall from many ages past. Further on, an aperture in the forest's mass showed a glimpse of the opposite side of the vale, where scattered pools of sunlight illuminated the mauve and orange hues of the Wicklow Mountains. How majestic they looked in the gloaming, their great peaks obscured in a covering of delicate clouds.

The road soon led us to a clearing where the heavy undergrowth fell away revealing the valley's gentler slopes. Straight ahead, and showing behind an ancient pile of mouldering stonework, I could make out the contours of an abandoned settlement. Fr. Moynihan saw it too, and pointing towards the sombre remains of a dilapidated bell tower, he suggested we should enter the grounds by scaling a stile, that still showed clearly in the crumbling wall by the roadside. While some of the baying hounds had lost interest and fallen back, a determined group of them continued their rowdy charge in front of us. I could sense their tension as with flared nostrils they bounded headlong over the opening in the embankment. We all made for the same spot, with the monk reaching the mildewed stile first. Then turning on his heels, he grasped Sean by both arms before demanding –

"Now think carefully. Are you sure it was here that the children found her? It will be dark soon enough, and we must find her before others do. A child's eye can often be mistaken."

"Yes, Father, I am certain. It was during this afternoon that they were playing here amongst the tombstones. Oh I know they should not have been anywhere outside the safety of the village boundaries, but none of us knew they were missing. It appears they had sneaked out through the gates when McIntyre had allowed a carriage to pass through. I'm afraid the graveyard is a popular playground for the young folk, and has been these last few Summers, before these killings began. It was only when their hysterical screams were heard clamouring up the road, that some of the trades folk rode out and brought them back to safety. They were so distraught that I doubt if they will ever recover from such a shock."

"Then I should warn you, Sean, and Cathy, that if you ever knew Nan or held her dearly, now is the moment to return to your homes. A corpse is never a pleasant sight and I would not have you visited by the same nightmares as the little ones. These soldiers are hardened by battle and have the stomachs for such carnage, but I'll wager even they may find their mettle tested."

The bleak honesty of his words sent shivers down our spines.

"But we are both not afraid, Father!" protested Sean. "Nan was our friend and we would not abandon her to such a lonely fate, or forsake her dignity in this dreadful place. What manner of man would you think me if I bolted now like a frightened hare? We owe it to Nan and her father, and will not shirk from the task. For pity's sake, let us come with you!"

"I never doubted the courage or compassion of your hearts, Sean, and it is clear you are quite resolved to see it through. Alright then – but stay well back behind me and Mr. Parsons, and keep within an arm's length of the soldier's muskets. Be alert, and do not touch anything. Is the cart ready, Daniel?"

I nodded in assent as the wagon took up its place beside the roadside.

"Then let us go."

As the hooded monk clambered over the wet stile, I signalled to one of the redcoats to keep back the small group of stragglers that had followed us from the village. How odd a creature is man, I thought, that despite his dread of unspeakable terrors, his fears are as nothing compared to the power of his insatiable curiosity.

Clearing the wall, we found ourselves amongst a

cluster of overgrown headstones, where moss and lichen clung deep within the cracks and crevices of the carvings. With the passage of time these noble broken slabs had fallen forward, and grass and briars now hid their melancholy forms. An avenue of ancient yew trees hung above them, casting deep shadows along a neglected pathway, as the cleric's robes moved swiftly along their verges. Here and there large mounds of masonry retained the outlines of broken sepulchres, where arch and pillar still gave semblance to their former statures. A Celtic cross of spiral design sat atop several of these hallowed vaults. Sadly some of their entrances had been smashed or pulled away, revealing large holes leading downwards into the catacombs.

I shuddered as we passed these silent black openings and I could not suppress a deep nervousness every time my back was turned to them. What it was that made me fearful I could not say, but the smell of a rank, stale odour that rose from several of these tombs, undoubtedly fuelled my imagination. A rustling of leaves made me jump, and as I scrutinized the dark recesses of the trees I could make out many dense inky objects darting quickly through the thick grass – seemingly involved in a good deal of mischief. A feeling of repugnance rose within me as I realized that these were the lightening movements of copious rats. One of the soldiers in front of me cursed as he narrowly avoided treading on a rodent which ran across his path. The further we advanced the more it appeared that the whole area was heaving with them.

The whimpering calls of the fevered canines drew Fr. Moynihan's attention to the nave of a deserted chapel below the bell tower. The corbelled gothic windows had long since lost their roof, but most of the structure remained intact, including the transepts on either side. He crossed around to the back of the church and then disappeared under the covering of several trees, where the noise of the dogs was most pronounced. We sped after him to the rear of the building until we came upon his stationary figure, which stood rigid and motionless.

The priest's gaze was transfixed on something before him, and it was then – oh sweet Christ of mercy, that even now I find it diabolical to relate – but it was then that we all saw what had held his attention. Hanging by a short rope from the gnarled branch of a beech tree, a revolting vision presented itself. A barely discernible head and torso of a dead woman, was all that could be seen from under a solid teeming mass of frenzied rats, whose movements produced a swarm of vermin all over her limbs. Scores of them formed a writhing pillar of horror that stretched from where her toes barely touched the ground, up along the whole body, over her head, and back up the cord, where they ran along the tree's arteries. It was like a swarm of wasps roused to anger and intent on harming their prey. I retched in my throat as I felt my gorge rise, and a sharp spasm spread across my back and shoulders, where my muscles contracted with tension. Nothing had prepared me for so hellish an apparition and I fought desperately inside myself to conceal my terror from those around me.

Sean and Cathy set up a wail of anguish and would have broken forward, but were held back by some of the soldiers whose instinct was to guard them from further distress. Fr. Moynihan also commanded them to stay back with an imperious gesture of his arm, and rousing myself from my shock I ordered several of the redcoats to discharge their firearms high above the rodents to disperse them. The blasts from their muskets exploded with a deafening charge, and the startled creatures scattered in every direction. Wave upon wave of the odious beasts dropped to the ground, and the black monk stamped furiously at them, shouting in rage as he waded through their ranks. The man's tenacity impressed me and in a few seconds he had succeeded in clearing the body of all obstacles. He motioned me to come closer, and nauseous though I was, I found courage to approach the tree.

"The light is fast fading, Daniel. Have your men ready to cut her down at my instruction, but give me some moments to examine her first. I will be as swift as possible. We have been fortunate in some respects."

Without another word he proceeded to investigate the body with a courage I could only admire, scrutinizing the victim at close quarters. His roving eye moved up and down the corpse with the detachment of a scholar looking over a document, and I could see that he was indeed collating information. The flesh had been brutally lacerated with mutilations to the stomach and breasts. Certain markings and wounds caused the cleric to pause longer, but in the dim light I could not distinguish one lesion from another. Strips of torn flesh could be observed where the rats had done their worst, and I had to turn away frequently where my senses became sickened at the sight. The priest then dropped to the ground and began a thorough search of the earth below the victim's feet. In rapid succession I saw him lunge forward with his hands and snap up several objects which he then held up to his eye for closer examination. Whatever they were I could see that they animated his interest greatly, and placing them in the deep pockets of his garment he continued to scour the area on his hands and knees. At times he resembled a pack hound – so intense was his concentration. When he had ceased his endeavours he stood upright and approached me.

"Now – get her down, and have your men escort the body to Glenboyne. While I have learnt much, it would be beneficial to us to find a surgeon in the village to help determine both the cause and nature of the wounds. The moon has already risen and we must not linger further in the darkness of this place."

I needed no prompting, and in an instant two of the infantrymen had severed the rope, while proceeding to wrap her remains in disused flaxen bags, which they had brought from the wagon. Experienced though they were, I saw the look of consternation in their faces at the savagery of the attack, and slowly they proceeded to labour across the graveyard with the weight of Nan Harold between them. A sudden vehemence arose in Sean as he broke from behind the soldiers and prostrated himself before Fr. Moynihan, clasping the Benedictine's robes in a vice-grip of violent passion.

"It's that monster Buckley who has done this! Him and his accursed Hellfire Club atop Montpelier Hill. They are in league with the Devil, Father, – all of them! You must believe me. Many have heard it in the dead of night – some monstrous creature lurking in the woods! The villagers pretend it is a lone wolf – but I tell you it is something far worse. Conjured by Buckley and his fires on the mountainside. Why look! Even now – I can see the flames upon the hilltop! Look, Father! Tell him Catherine! Tell him!" It was true. None of us had noticed it before, but as we turned our eyes skyward in the increasing darkness, we could see, some miles distant, a dull red glow flickering atop the valley's summit.

"No, Sean. For the love of God hold your tongue – you don't know what you are saying – not here – you must not say such things."

Cathy's blond hair swept across his pallid face as she tried to disengage him from the monk's tunic. He turned his wild blue eyes on her, and in an indignant tone of voice he pulled away from her gentle caresses.

"And why not? We all know it's the truth. Would you have me pretend otherwise? What do you think got Nan and the others? It is here... I know it is here... I heard the Reverend Hearne say so last week... save us, Father... save us!"

The priest towered above him and rested his great hands upon the youth's heaving shoulders.

"You are deeply upset, Sean, by what you have seen. I understand fully your rage and turmoil, but you must calm yourself. Cathy is right – if you have anything to say – do not utter it here. Hold your council awhile until we have reached the refuge of safer walls, where you can unburden your heart in quieter surroundings. The very stones and mortar of these tombs may have eyes and ears of their own, and if you have suspicions to impart – do so later to myself or Mr. Parsons. Now trust in your friends and God – they will give you strength and support."

As we departed the graveyard, Wilkinson told me that he had already prepared the cart and its grim cargo. Proceeding along the road, the Corporal and his men took up the rear of our company, and within no time we had gained the outskirts of the village. As we re-entered the turnpike gate Private Saunders was instructed that the remains should be removed to the premises of a local doctor, and I agreed with Fr. Moynihan that we should visit this physician on the following morning. I was never so pleased as when we reached the civil usage of the Eagle Tavern's doors, where the landlord had the grace to provide us with a small but welcome repast. A splenetic Harry Maguire scolded his daughter for her absence, but hugged her in equal measure for her spirit in accompanying us.

As I ate I pondered over Sean's words. What indeed were the fires at the top of the mountain? What was The Hellfire Club? Did it even exist? Rumours of the possible activities of such a club had reached Dublin Castle some months ago – but information on it was scant. Had it any connection to these appalling deaths? And what was Sir Jack Buckley's involvement, if any?

Of the victims themselves I knew only their names, which had been passed to me by the authorities in Dublin Castle. Mary O'Dwyer was the first casualty, followed thereafter by Therese Mulholland, and now, as I knew, both joined in death by Nan Harold, and her father. But of their lives and place in this small community - I knew nothing.

Overwhelmed with exhaustion, both I and Fr. Moynihan retired to our separate rooms. Closing my eyelids I felt sure I could hear the cries of distant wolves carried along by the wind outside, which chaffed fretfully at my window pane, until its echoes faded into a sleep of unquiet dreams.

V

A FELT BRIMMED HAT

The following morning, both I and Fr. Moynihan breakfasted early and enquired from the innkeeper directions to the surgeon's house. To our amazement Harry Maguire started chuckling to himself, with a whimsical grin breaking across his lips. He saw our confusion and proceeded to explain the source of his amusement.

"Why, that great lump Hannon is hardly a doctor, Mr. Parsons. More of a horse surgeon if you ask me. At least that is what is thought of him locally. A worse practitioner of healing it would be hard to find. You'll never guess what he prescribed last week as a cure for the Reverend Hearne's baldness? He told him to fill up a goat's bladder with human urine, then hang it over a fire to dry, and to grind it down later as a powder. To this he was supposed to add raw onion, a cup of buttermilk to make a paste, and then rub the whole concoction onto his scalp. Needless to say the esteemed minister is as bald as ever this week, with a notable rash to the dome of his skull – not to mention the stink! Perhaps I speak too harshly of him, and I know Hannon means well, but I'd be wary of his medical advice."

He broke off laughing here, and I could see the hilarity in what he described.

I barely showed a smile, but Fr. Moynihan was less subtle than I, and his deep booming laugh broke forth and filled the room like a clamorous bell. As I would discover, the Benedictine's inherent (and sometimes irreverent) sense of humour was one of his strongest personal traits – and it was hard to listen to that marvellous sound without feeling its infectious joy. I realised too with some dismay, that it was the first laughter I had heard since arriving in Glenboyne.

"Anyway, Mr. Parsons, it being Saturday and market day, you should have no difficulty in finding his cottage. Since these recent killings and fearful of an attack, you can understand that many of the traders have almost ceased their business, but a persistent few continue to sell their wares. My daughter will most likely be there collecting whatever victuals she can for me, and with so little available she gets to the stalls as early as she can. If you should lose your way, I'm sure she can direct you. Otherwise cut straight across the market square and you will find the track past Maul's Tower, where he lives along the riverside."

As we left the confines of the tavern's warmth Wilkinson greeted us outside and re-assured me that he had posted a guard at Dr. Hannon's abode, and he was ready to accompany us to the surgeon's premises. The zealous Corporal reported to me that he had borrowed some horses from the village tradesmen, and conducted a further search for Private Taylor early at dawn, – but that the hollow had given up no trace of him. We both agreed that further resources would be needed, and I instructed him to send word to Colonel Butler at Rathfarnham Castle to release a company of men with some cavalry as soon as possible to Glenboyne. Wilkinson advised me that there were a number of battalions stationed at this fortress, which was normally two day's march from the village. But he stressed that a scout had told him that the recent storm had caused a mud-slide, which was partially blocking the entrance to Kelly's Gorge below The Giant's Grave. He felt a single messenger might be able to get through, but we were cut off from Dublin temporarily. It could be some days before re-enforcements arrived. Worse still, he explained that Harkin the coach driver was having difficulty in getting the village blacksmith to repair quickly the damaged chassis of the coach, as it seems he was most busily engaged in finishing some ironwork for a local aristocrat. Consequently, the axles might not be fixed for several days. But I realized that this meant we were without any effective transport, and so I gave the Corporal the authority to commandeer any further horses he could from the village occupants or local farmers – as otherwise we would be without proper mobility. To this end I placed a purse of coins in his palm, and told him to hire the horses where he could. He was not to use coercion or threats to attain them – it was crucial we kept the local populace on our side. In the meantime the strength of our legs would have to suffice.

As we proceeded along the main street, several bent figures with parcels of huddled rags could be seen moving in what we guessed must be the direction of the village square. So instead of crossing down towards the turnpike gate, we turned right up a laneway and stumbled upon the market-place. In truth it was not a proper square, more of an ill-fitting quadrangle, with broken buildings and crumbling edifices on all sides. The only structure of note was a three-storied grain house, built from weathered granite blocks, and intercepted throughout by high arched windows, masked by wooden shutters. A hauling device and a score of oaken barrels were gathered around its entrance. The ground was paved in irregular cobblestones, except for the centre of the area, which opened into a large tract of muck and waste ground. Here there was found a smattering of old carts and broken wagons, where a group of shabby tradesmen and farmers had arrived to ply their goods in the open air. There were bushels of dirty hay, battered copper pots, bales of tinder sticks, sacks of barley, rushlights and candlewax, barrels of lime, scythes, winnowing trays, flails, and all manner of implements for sale or barter.

Many a cold and hostile eye followed our steps across the expanse of the market-place. The murmurs of the tradesfolk fell silent, and dozens of sallow faces turned down their mouths in haughty disgust at our presence. Several stray dogs that had been feeding on scraps snapped and snarled at us, as though voicing the general animosity of the crowd towards our company. It was a singularly uncomfortable experience.

Of food there was little to be seen, with the exception of a lone farmer, who had laid out an assortment of dead chickens on a wooden box. He was surrounded by a mob of hungry street urchins who were determined to steal away with one of his poultry. Close by, I spotted Cathy chiding the children, several of whom she seemed to know. Next to them a tiny barefoot girl was sitting alone playing with a stick amongst the dirt. With a series of oaths and profanations the farmer drove the little brats away, until one of them ran headlong into the butt of Wilkinson's musket. Picking himself up quickly it was not long before the young rascal had caught up with the other boys, who from a distance could not resist a parting outburst. A few of the bolder ones picked up stones and hurled them at us, while screeching at the top of their lungs –

"English redcoat scum! Get out of our country you bloody tyrants!"

One of the soldiers seemed ready to give them chase, but before we could react a thunderous clatter of hooves and the shrieking of many horses burst upon our ears from the other side of the square. A magnificent black coach pulled by four black steeds broke across the cobblestones, followed by a retinue of various horses all mounted by either manservants or several armed riders. Resplendent red plumes danced atop the horses' heads, and two footmen dressed in red and silver livery stood perched behind the vehicles' rooftop. The coachman (if such he can be called) was a stocky dwarf with a small thick neck and black goatee beard. He had a surly look about him and cracked his whip viciously against the creatures' backs. Sweat and foam exuded from their bridles as they charged with breakneck speed towards us.

In a moment of horror I realized that the transport was tearing uncontrollably towards the little girl playing on the ground, and was sure to strike her in a matter of seconds. The pounding of the wheels and the groan of the axles vibrated in my ears, and seized by instinct I dived recklessly forward, just in time to whip her from the danger. Clasped tightly together, we rolled in a heap for several feet along the dusty earth. Had we not cleared its path in time, we would both have been torn limb from limb by the razor-like action of the straked wheels.

Several screams rose from the marketplace and a gathering of onlookers ran to our aid. One amongst them was the mother of the girl, who ran frantically towards me expecting the worst. I handed her the child who was now crying, and she hugged it close to her chest, while thanking me it seemed with some reluctance verging on petulance.

But my ire now turned on the coach, which along with its party had come to a grinding halt just feet from where I rose from the ground. Fr. Moynihan followed behind me as I bounded towards the dwarf, who had dismounted from the conveyance and was closely examining the wheels.

"You there!" I exploded. "What the hell do you mean driving like that? You could have killed that child with such reckless behaviour. Are you listening? Did you not see her in front of you? Get up when I address you! You are speaking to an officer of the King's Law!"

The small figure got up off his knees, and glared savagely at me with a look of the deepest contempt.

"Child, did you say? What childer was dat now? I did not spy any little one on de road. But it is certain hard to see dem, especially when dey run out of a sudden from nowhere – ah sure ye know yourself."

"You know perfectly well the child I am referring to – that little girl whose legs you could have crushed," I pointed, " and you will address me as Sir!"

"Oh well, Sir. In dat case I am sorry for yer truuble. But I assure ye I did not see her, and I would na a harmed a hair on her little head had I known she was dere. God's truut. Me mastuur ye see... he has pressing matuurs in de town... and well... he needs to reach his destination wid all speed, udderwise me mastuur... "

But I cut across him.

"You are an impudent rascal, and no matter how urgent your business is, it does not give you leave to risk life and limb along the way. Who is your master? I would speak with him."

As soon as I had uttered these words, a white hand with a lustrous gold ring swung open the coach door, and a formidable voice resounded from within.

"I am his master, Mr. Parsons, and you will address me as Sir Jack Buckley!"

I was not prepared for such a revelation, and the utterance of the name sent a chill of revulsion coursing through my veins. I thought of my dear father who had always taught me to face and do the thing I feared the most, and in this moment that sage advice gave me some comfort, as I took a step back and tried to compose myself for the extraordinary figure that now came forward into the sunshine. My heart pounded as my body became tense.

Alighting from the vehicle he stood intimidatingly close to me, and fixed my eye with an icy gaze. He was very tall – I calculated he was about six foot three inches (a full three inches taller than myself), with a lean sinuous figure, and muscular bony hands. In one of these he held a silver cane, and in the other a pair of white satin gloves. His face was strong and handsome with distinct aristocratic features, including a cleft chin, and a perfectly proportioned nose. But it was his eyes that drew the most attention. The left orb was a brilliant cobalt blue, but as if in mocking contrast to it, his right eye revealed a startlingly mutated white eyeball, where a scar, disfiguring his face, ran from his forehead across his right eye socket, to just above the cheekbone. Therefore, despite his good looks this abnormality, along with a cruel fixed mouth, gave him a malignant appearance.

His grey hair, which fell to his shoulders in luxurious curls, seemed prematurely aged for a man in his late thirties, as I esteemed him to be. On his head he wore a wide brimmed hat of black felt, which he hung low at one corner of his forehead to partially hide his deformity. He wore a coat and waistcoat of the finest black satin, with both embellished from cravat to knee by a long string of buttons, decorated with gold twist. Exotic floral patterns of red satin formed a design along his waistcoat, and in the fashion of the time his coat sleeves were generously turned back to form a funnel or 'boot cuff', buttoned just above the elbow. A pair of dark knee-length breeches resting above silk stockings and black squared-toed shoes completed his attire.

His immediate appearance caused consternation amongst the traders, several of whom hid quickly behind carts and barrels, desperate to avoid him. What manner of man was he, I wondered, that could inspire more loathing than a British redcoat? I signalled to several of the soldiers to stand close by me in case of a possible altercation.

"Well, well, and what have we here?" he sneered. "A remarkable sight indeed! Who would have thought it? An English official keen to do his duty accompanied by a black monk! Can you believe it boys? A black monk I tell you! And no ordinary monk either!"

He shouted out these last words to the mounted manservants behind him, who laughed and sniggered in expected response. Then turning on my person he addressed me with profound vehemence.

"How dare you speak to one of my servants in such a fashion? The base effrontery of it! I would have you shackled and flogged for such an impertinence. Did he not tell you that he could not see her? And this Benedictine dog at your side – are you not aware it is strictly forbidden for any catholic blasphemers to practise their witchcraft without punishment or exile? Or do you not know this, Mr. Parsons, being a newcomer to this isle? He has no right to show his face in Glenboyne. Get him out of here at once, or I will see to it that he is put in the stocks and left there."

I was fuming inside but was determined not to let him goad me into anger, as seemed his main intention. A cooler response issued from my lips.

"As you are acquainted with my name, I will return to you the same compliment, Sir Buckley, and as a standing gentleman your title will be treated with the utmost respect. But I must make it clear that this monk is not practising his faith, and is under my protection to help me with an investigation into the heinous murders of this community. He has an official pardon from the Lord Lieutenant's office and no one shall lay a finger upon him. To that end I have a warrant that gives me full power to search every dwelling in this district, whether hut, barn, or castle. It is signed by the Prime Sergeant himself with his seal – here – perhaps you would like to read it?"

Amazed at my own courage, I took the parchment from my satchel and thrust it into his hand. He clutched at it and with probing eyes he read the content greedily, before throwing it back at me.

"Then you have wasted your journey," he spat. "We already know what caused those deaths. The fields and woods hereabouts are overrun with starving wolves, driven down from the mountains in search of food. They have arrived early this winter, and their packs have already savaged dozens of my livestock. There is nothing more lethal than the incisor tooth of a wolf's jaw as it rips through flesh and sinew. I am amazed that your clever officials in Dublin Castle do not read the reports about these things. Two of my own workers were attacked by them and my huntsmen have shot eight in the last week. Isn't this so, Mick?"

His pointed question was directed to one of the burly thugs on horseback behind the coach, who I noticed fingered a firearm most nervously.

"That's right, Master Jack," he acquiesced, "you tell him, Sir!"

I ignored this crude interruption. But my instincts told me that his explanation may have been a deception to deflect me from entering his stately abode. Should this be so I would play his game and draw him out.

"Perhaps you are right, Sir Buckley," I pretended, "and I thank you for that information. In fact, what you have described could turn out to be most fortuitous, as it would help me considerably to see some of these dead carnivores. By doing so I could either eliminate them from my investigations, or alternatively return to my superiors in Dublin with evidence of the cause of the killings. You would have no objection I am sure if I were to visit Montpelier Hall to examine their carcasses? Their bodies might still retain some traces of human remains, which would lend great weight to your argument."

His keen blue eye glared suspicion at me, and with a malicious grin he said,

"Oh, that won't be necessary – you see we burned them last night in case they spread disease. They are vermin after all and one cannot be too careful."

"Is that so?" I replied, "yes – you took every sensible precaution I am sure... but maybe you could keep the next wolf you catch and allow us to cut it open? After all, where there are eight wolves – there are bound to be many more in the area. Even their charred ashes might reveal something to help determine the facts. You see, I am worried that it may not be an animal which is responsible for these attacks, and if this is so the perpetrators could be hiding anywhere, even in the woods about your property. I could not have it on my conscience, Sir Buckley, if you were attacked and I had done nothing to prevent it. I think a search about Montpelier would put my mind greatly at ease. It would be a short and cursory visit, I assure you, and we will keep disruption to a minimum. Besides, I cannot perceive how a wolf could tie a corpse to a tree in a graveyard!"

This last comment enraged the same mounted brute that had intervened so rudely some moments earlier, who, pulling back the flintlock on his musket, spat on the ground close to my feet.

"You seem to do a lot of thinking, don't you, Mr. Englishman?"

"SILENCE, Kearney!" roared Buckley.

Then adjusting the brim of his hat, and seeming to adopt an entirely different approach, he lowered his voice to a softer tone, and with a surreptitious smile he said –

"Come, come, Mr. Parsons! You do not need to wave seals and documents at us. If it is your desire to visit my lands, you are of course welcome to do so, and we shall assist you in any way we can. After all, we are a hospitable people here in Glenboyne. Aren't we lads? As you will appreciate my estate makes great demands upon my time, and with the feast of Samhain nearly upon us, the Halloween hunt must soon be organised. But when you are ready my servant here, Lundy, will provide transport and safe passage for you to Montpelier's grounds. He is often in the village attending to my needs, and will make himself known to you. Isn't that right, Lundy? Isn't it?"

Here he aimed a well-judged kick at the midget's posterior, where he landed a blow that knocked him several steps forward. Some of the horsemen gave tongue to loud laughter, but when the dwarf regained his footing, I never saw such a look of daggers as he pierced his master with a murderous glare. But wisdom bade him stay silent.

"We have lingered here long enough, and I must be about my business. Lundy! Resume your seat, and mind how you go. It seems there was a girl after all, as Mr. Parsons said. What wretched carelessness of you, Lundy! Ho there! Up! Away!"

With a parting scoff he re-ascended the vehicle, and rapped zealously on the rooftop with his splendid cane. From the coach window he stared at me intensely, with a face of perfect poise, but the hatred in that left eye was palpable and voracious. Then the horses plunged and shook their manes as the great black wheels jolted forward into motion. In an instant the conveyance, the elegant beasts, and the party of mounted riders all disappeared beneath a cloud of fine dust and swirling leaves. Some moments later they had traversed the square and were gone. I was very relieved that this close encounter had come to pass, but I knew there would be others in the days ahead.

"Thank you, Mr. Parsons. Your quick response saved young Tilly from certain death, and it was an act of great courage. I just wanted you to know how grateful we are – her family appreciate it deeply. Do not think too harshly of them for failing to express this directly – as they cannot be seen to do so. I know you will understand, and they will remember what you have done."

It was the voice of Cathy Maguire that spoke to me, as her bashful green eyes were raised to meet mine. Before turning to leave, she graced me with the sweetest of smiles, as I stood there enchanted by her gesture. A string of coral pearls could not have shone more brightly than the radiant warmth of that charming smile. Fr. Moynihan also squeezed my arm and with perfect sincerity said quietly –

"Thank you, Daniel."

VI

THE PLEASUREABLE DR. HANNON

There was time enough I knew to discuss later what we had seen and heard, but desirous to ban Buckley's presence momentarily from my mind, I determined we would focus on reaching the surgeon's house soon, and quickly we made with haste across the open market-place. I was concerned that Fr. Moynihan might react badly to the goading he had just suffered at Buckley's hands, or that it might embitter him against assisting me. But his temperament did not seem that way inclined, as he strode purposefully beside me, his head held high, and maintaining a dignified silence. This was both impressive and encouraging.

Beyond the grain house we took a stony track that led down a gentle slope towards the sluggish river bordering one side of the village. Although I calculated it to be a quarter of a mile distant, Maul's Tower seemed much closer, rising from the marsh and reed beds as though it had taken root and grown out of the earth. Clearly it had been built along the water's edge to act as a fortress in troubled days gone by, and this path must once have approached its entrance. A handful of dingy cabins now lined the route, until we came to a tidy thatched cottage, set in off the way by a latched gate and low stone wall. The building must have been expanded recently, as a lean-to on the right side of the structure showed a freshly thatched roof and clean plastered mud. The eaves of this extension were below that of the main roof, and a swing-door provided independent access to this side of the cottage. The only other outhouse was a wooden barn, where I was pleased to see the tricorne of a redcoat's hat resting against the wall and leaning on his musket. It was Private Saunders.

As we slipped through the latched gate, a frail old lady in a large Irish shawl was pushed with some haste out of the swing-door, and deposited unceremoniously onto the garden path. She turned to ask a question, but a clutch of stubby fingers were already in the process of closing the door on her. Before she could frame a sentence a pompous voice issued from the entrance.

"Not at all Mrs. McDonagh. Any time. Just keep using the poultice and the inflammation should go down. Bye, bye, now. Take care. Pleasure!"

The door slammed so fast that had she placed her hand anywhere near it, it would surely have been amputated. As soon as she set eyes upon us, she hid herself inside her shawl, and passed out the latched gate, back up the laneway towards the village. I surmised that this surgeon was likely to have examined not only Nan Harold's corpse, but that he may have been the last person to view all of the deceased victims before their burials. Wilkinson saw to it that a handful of infantrymen remained on the road until we had concluded our business. The swing-door was divided into an upper half and a lower half, both of which could open separately, depending on how the bolts were fastened. I seized at the black iron knocker and rapped firmly for a response.

A cough and splutter, followed by the sound of shuffling boots, soon announced the person within. An iron bar was thrown back, and the top half of the door sprang open with such violence that it grazed the sides of my hair.

"Now, now, Mrs. McDonagh. What is it this time? Couldn't you wait until I... good heavens! What is going on here? More redcoats! Now look – I've had about enough of this, do you understand? I'm trying to attend to my patients today. I'm a respectable doctor and your soldiers are scaring away my business. What do you mean blurting in on me unannounced? If you are that official come from Dublin wishing to ask me questions – there is a proper time and place for doing so."

This outburst came from a fat little man with an unctuous face and bilious expression. His cheeks were of a pinkish-red and a sprinkling of light perspiration rested on his forehead, which he wiped frequently. A bald head crowned his brow, save for some limp grey hair that hung lankly from his temples. Two piggish eyes and an unflattering squat nose completed his distinctly unattractive features. His figure and bearing suggested he had already seen his fiftieth birthday, but by what margin I could not guess.

"I'm afraid it is not that simple, Dr. Hannon, and I have no desire to disturb the course of your work. But it is imperative that we ask several questions. You have nothing to fear – it will only take up a few moments of your time. Is there somewhere private where we could talk alone? Perhaps inside?" I queried.

A second door was heard to open from within, and a shrill, irksome voice called out over the surgeon's shoulder.

"Who is it dear? Did I hear voices? Is it Mr. Balfour with his gout again? Don't keep him standing there – you know how it vexes him!"

"No, my love. It is not Mr. Balfour. Just a few callers from the city making some enquiries. I can handle it, and I've told you BEFORE not to come in when I'm seeing a patient. Now run along my darling, and close the door into the kitchen, so that I can speak to the gentlemen properly."

"Oh well, if they have come all that way, why don't you bring them in for a dram of whiskey, dear? There is an awful draught coming through that door, and I'm sure they must be tired."

On hearing this comment from his wife the stout figure surprised and shocked us, when he began to contort his face into a frightful display of ill temper. The depth of his reaction suggested that bad blood existed between the couple.

"BLAST AND BOTHERATION WOMAN!" he yelled. "I've told you what to do. Now stop interfering and let me deal with it!"

A curt slam from inside suggested that Mrs. Hannon heeded his advice, and the clenched teeth of her husband were now transformed into a mawkish smile.

"Goodness me, gentlemen. You must forgive her unseemly manners. She gets quite excited some times when we have visitors, and likes to be involved in everything. But of course, she is quite right. It would be a pleasure to assist you where I can in your enquiries. An absolute pleasure! Please, do come in, as I'm not expecting Mr. Balfour for some time yet."

We entered a plain snug whitewashed room, where a small open hearth gave life to a roaring turf fire. A settlebed sat nearby with its high wooden back nestled into a deep alcove, and on its long bench lay an apathetic cat, which shared the space with a pile of mouldering leather books. Standing opposite, an oaken dresser showed evidence of his practice, in the shape of many glass phials containing medicinal compounds, sitting neatly in rows beside a mortar and pestle.

"And now, Sir, you have the advantage of me. I

don't believe we have been introduced. What did you say your name was? Mr. eh... Mr?..."

"Daniel Parsons is my name, and this is Fr. Moynihan my travelling companion."

"Delighted to meet you, Mr. Parsons – it's a pleasure to be sure. And you too, Father. What an absolute pleasure to have your company in these troubled times. Now what is it you wish to ask me? Is it an ailment that bothers you? Back pain no doubt?"

"No," I replied, "what can you tell us about the cause of Nan Harold's death? Or the death of Mary O'Dwyer and Therese Mulholland? That is chiefly want we want to know."

He shot up from his chair, knocking it backwards in an apoplexy of rage.

"LEAVE ME ALONE!" he screamed.

"LEAVE ME ALONE, DAMN YOU!" – bringing his fist down on the table. I was sure he must burst a blood vessel.

"So you've come to trick me? Is that your game? Come to laugh at my supposed failings like the villagers did? They tried to say that Mary and Therese were still alive when they first found them – and had I arrived at the scenes earlier that I might have saved them! What slander and lies! They were already dead long before

I got there. I am not a miracle worker. My God! Their flesh... it was torn so badly, mangled and ripped... over, and over, and over. I could barely find the strength to touch it."

He raised his clenched hands in the air, examining them like a madman.

Then covering his eyes, he collapsed in a heap back into the chair where he sobbed convulsively. This outburst appeared as baffling as it was disproportionate. I wondered if he suffered from a chronic nervous disposition, or was this some elaborate charade for reasons he did not wish to share? For the moment I was inclined to believe the former, while maintaining an open mind on the latter possibility. I leant forward slowly so as not to startle him.

"Calm yourself, Dr. Hannon. You are much mistaken, and please accept my apologies for any upset caused. We are not here to blame you for anything. Far from it – we have heard nothing but the highest of praise for your excellent skills. Isn't that so, Father? No doubt you did everything possible – your reputation and integrity are not on trial here. Trust me."

A beady eye with a hint of a sly glance peeped out from behind his hands, but he continued to say nothing.

"I know it is distressing to recount the details, but you had I assume a chance to look at all the bodies individually? Will you share your findings?"

He lowered his palms and wiped his sweaty brow with a dirty rag.

"The highest of praise, did you say?" he gibbered.

"Most definitely," I pretended. "You are respected as a very fine surgeon. Why else would we set so much upon your opinion?"

I saw Fr. Moynihan cock one of his eyes at me, as he tried to restrain himself from laughing. He disguised it brilliantly by putting his hand across his mouth to affect a cough.

"Now take your time," I continued, "and we will bring you through it step by step. Would that be acceptable? Gather your thoughts and let us make a start."

"Well... eh... yes... I suppose... that is to say I suppose... I might remember certain observations that I made. I'll do my best – but don't push, mind! There was so much mud, blood, and tissue. My Lord! The tissue!"

"Are you ready?"

He nodded sheepishly.

"Where is Nan Harold's body now?"

"Well... ah... she is... that is, she is lying in the outhouse, Sir, which I keep in the garden. She has been laid out and cleaned to join her father in burial tomorrow at the Reverend Hearne's chapel. Both will be interred within the grounds as is the custom. That is to say, and begging your pardon, Father, they were of the same congregation, if you follow my drift?"

"You mean they were Protestants?"

"Exactly so, Mr. Parsons."

"You had a chance to examine her body? What did you find?" I queried.

His eyes began to twitch as he continued to mop his soaked forehead, and he assumed I felt, a rather affected pose of self-importance.

"She was assaulted feverishly and had suffered a fatal blow to the top of her head resulting in internal bleeding and the puncturing of the skin. Are you familiar with the trachelian muscles, Sir? They are located near the base of the neck, and I found them to have been sliced through by a serrated object or objects unknown. If it was a weapon that caused such destruction I was unable to identify it, but it was most savage. From below her chest the entire lower body had been torn out – removed. She had been hacked to pieces. Nor was it possible to discover if she had one attacker, several, or even if it were the work of human hands, animals, or... "

"Yes? What?" I asked.

"Perhaps some other diabolical entity," came his chilling reply.

"Let us stick with what we know, doctor. How did Geoffrey Harold die?"

"Again he suffered from a severe injury to the skull, either from a fall or deliberate blow – but he had no other wounds and was not cut up."

"And for the others – Mary O'Dwyer and Therese Mulholland – did they die in a similar manner to Nan? Slashed violently? With equal intensity?"

"I'm afraid so," he concurred.

"But what was it? Do you think it was a wolf?"

"In truth I really could not say, Mr. Parsons," he said hesitantly.

"I assume that as a man of medicine you completely reject any suggestion of it being something unnatural? There has already been mention in the village of an unseen beast – some terrifying presence that threatens the community. We even had an unsettling experience ourselves when we came through Kelly's Gorge. There was a deadly creature of considerable size which attacked us in that hollow – isn't this so, Father?"

"Very true," agreed the Benedictine, "and it left large hoof marks!"

"Surely you don't mean the DEVIL'S WORK, Father? SAINTS PRESERVE US!" gasped the surgeon as he made the Sign of the Cross above his chest.

"I did not say that, Dr. Hannon," replied the monk. "I only remarked that something had left unusually large imprints at the scene of the assault. What it was remains a mystery."

"Have you witnessed anything peculiar yourself?" I enquired.

The sweating figure swallowed hard and shook nervously at the question.

"I will not deny that strange things have been sighted in recent weeks, and that sounds too awful to contemplate have haunted the fields and woods hereabouts. No one will stir out of doors after dark, and some locals will swear to seeing... well... some type of black thing, large and powerful, lurking and hiding in the shadowy groves. It is hard not to be influenced by their persistent stories. But I chide them all for such irresponsible chatter, and argue that there must be some other explanation."

"Very wise words," I exclaimed, "and common sense should always prevail where possible. One final question – what age were these three women?"

"Mary I believe was nineteen, and Therese only twenty one. Nan was the youngest of the three in fact. She was only eighteen. Such wasted lives."

"You have been most helpful, doctor. And now we must take our leave of you. Fr. Moynihan would like to pay a short visit to the deceased and say a prayer over her. You don't mind if he does this I hope? It will only take a moment."

"Why not at all, Mr. Parsons. I would consider it a pleasure to have a prayer said for her soul. An absolute pleasure!"

With an irresistible impulse to get rid of us, he rose from his chair and quickly conducted us to the swing door. While I was never normally quick to judge a person's character I could not ignore the marked uneasiness in the man's behaviour. Was he a facile perspirer with a secret to hide, or a genuine victim of intense anxiety? He had us on the threshold before we could even catch our breaths.

"Thank you, Dr. Hannon. I hope we did not... "

"Not at all. Pleasure! Take care. Bye, bye, now."

The swing door slammed violently behind us before I could even turn to finish my sentence. It was the quickest exit I had ever experienced. With my words left hanging in the air we moved away from the lean-to and approached the wooden structure where the corpse lay. While the hooded clergyman made himself busy inside, I took the chance to congratulate Private Saunders on his excellent work in recent days. The black monk did not linger there for long however, and emerged some minutes later with a satisfied look upon his face. He approached me as I waited by the latched gate.

"He knows something – doesn't he, Father?" I suggested.

"You can be sure of it, Daniel! And he is scared too. What that information is I do not know, nor is he likely to give it up willingly if he feels threatened. But I'll wager that as we learn more in the coming days it will become less difficult to decipher what the pleasurable Dr. Hannon might be hiding."

VII

SIX SIDES OF A DICE

That afternoon I deemed it advisable to split our small numbers into two separate groupings with specific tasks. Firstly, Wilkinson would take several men with him to continue procuring as many horses as he could to give us greater freedom of movement until our coach was fully repaired. Private Taylor's disappearance and possible murder was weighing heavily upon my mind, and it was still my forlorn hope that should we gather enough steeds to mount – we might be able to return to the Gorge to search for him once more. I knew it was a large area to cover and that only a proper contingent of cavalry would have any realistic chance of locating him. Therefore I repeated to the Corporal that it was essential one of his riders should break through to Colonel Butler, telling him we were isolated, and to send relief immediately from Rathfarnham. I remained hopeful that the mudslide he had mentioned was only a partial blockage, and one that could be cleared. Finally, I directed him to find Lundy the dwarf, and to tell him that we would visit Montpelier Hall and his master, at first light of dawn the following morning.

Meanwhile, I would lead my group consisting of Fr. Moynihan, Private Saunders, and several other foot soldiers, in a sweeping perimeter along the banks of the river, as far as Maul's Tower, calling at every habitation to see if anyone could tell us anything about the recent killings. I reasoned that somebody must know something, if I could only get them to talk.

It was a thankless task, and as we traversed field and marsh, we spent four miserable hours climbing over walls, rapping at locked doors, stumbling into mud pools, and peering through broken windows. As soon as we were seen or heard approaching, men, women, and children would vanish like a drifting mist, fires were extinguished, and an eerie silence would envelop each dwelling. At one cabin we heard planks of wood and heavy furniture moved against the door to bar our entry, and nothing I could say resulted in the slightest movement from inside.

One farmer and his family actually fled across a field, and hid within the reed beds watching us like frightened deer. I knew if it came to it that I could force an entry and demand an interview, but heavy-handed tactics would win me no favours with these people, and it was not a strategy that I was prepared to consider.

As dusk began to threaten and the shadows lengthened, I felt it safer that we should start to return to the village soon. Hunger and fatigue had begun to tell on us, whilst the earlier pleasant sunshine had now given way to squally showers. I worried that darkness might not be far off, and so I pressed ahead with our tedious routine.

On the southern flank of the Norman edifice we discovered a hidden dirt track that led in meandering fashion to a sizeable promontory of land that skirted the banks of the river. This knoll was densely wooded and protruded like a separate headland, standing at a right angle to the water's flow. A dilapidated dwelling could be seen amongst the branches, almost lost to view behind large clumps of yellow ragwort and whortleberry bushes. A thin bead of smoke was the only proclamation of a possible soul inside. On the opposite side of this path, facing inland, the copse thickened into forest, and ran for miles towards the base of the glowering mountains.

Fr. Moynihan stopped abruptly and tilted his head as though straining to hear something.

"What is it, Father?"

"I'm not sure, Daniel. But listen! Do you hear it?"

I did.

Mixed above the sighing of the wind I could make out the doleful sobs of someone crying close by. The plaintive sound alternated between bursts of extreme wretchedness, to a more resigned whimpering moan. It was a haunting noise, and I felt sure from the intonation of its voice that it was a child in great distress.

"Over there, across the ditch, it's coming from behind that tree," I yelled.

We bounded over the ferns, and found behind the trunk of an ancient sycamore the huddled form of a small boy dressed in rags, who was crouched into a ball, with his head and face buried in his knees. He was so upset that he hardly noticed our approach. But when he did, he sprang up in desperate alarm and waved his arms frantically at us to block our advance.

"No! no! Ged iway from me! Ged iway from me!"

His face was contorted into an extraordinary set of spasms, with both eyes starting from their sockets in wild terror. Pressing his back against the hulk of the tree he seemed paralyzed and rigid with fear. Fr. Moynihan stretched out a comforting hand to calm him, but the result was a chorus of agonised screams. Undaunted the priest pressed forward, and wrapped his arms around the child in a warm embrace. The little figure shook and trembled as though seized with an ague, and his cries began to subside as he wept into the cleric's tunic.

"There now. Hush, hush, young fella... try to calm yourself. You are in safe hands – we are not going to harm you. It seems you've had a nasty shock! What is it that frightens you so?"

The priest held him affectionately in his arms while trying to engage him in conversation. This however proved difficult as he continued to shiver and hide himself amongst the folds of the monk's robes. But with a little more coaxing he slowly began to open his eyes and survey our faces.

"That's better – what a brave youngster you are. Now take a few deep breaths, in and out – and again. Good lad. Is that your home over there?" quizzed the Corkman.

The boy nodded in affirmation and pointed to the tumble-down dwelling.

"And what is it that has you so alarmed?" continued Fr. Moynihan.

The child's eyes resumed an extraordinary dread and darted from left to right as if half expecting to see something over our shoulders.

"I sawd it – out der!" he choked, pointing to the wood opposite.

"Saw it? Saw what?"

"De monster! De 'orrible monster!"
He broke down once more into tears and lamentations with his tiny hands quivering in the priest's massive palms.

"I was trying to ged home wid me dog, when it ran off into dem trees, an' like I tried t' follow 'im, bud when I got t' dose bushes, me dog started a barkin' an' screamin', an' I heard de monster squashin' im an killin' im. An' den I ran, 'cause I heard it cummin at me, hissin' n' roarin! So's I ran, an' I ran, til I fell at dis tree wid me leg hurtin'. Den I hid here cos I couldn' move na more! I niver made a sound an' I's was sure he'd git me – but he didn't cos I covered myseln wid leaves, luts of leaves!"

A shiver ran down my spine as he recounted these details, and a faint nausea crept over me. My eyes caught Fr. Moynihan's and he too betrayed a deep unease. But he disguised it with consummate skill and reassuringly said –

"Ah now, it was only a fox I'm sure. Don't be filling your head with spooks and fairies. Did you get a look at it? Can you describe it for us?"

But the little one shook his head assiduously, clearly unwilling or unable to recall the dreadful images.

"You are a very brave boy," I interposed, "but did you see where it went?" He dropped his head.

"What direction did it take?"

"Dunno," he blubbered. "I wanna go home. I dunno nuttin," and he clung once more to the monk's garments with an eager pleading in his eyes.

Wrapping the child tenderly within the folds of his black robe, the cleric requested that I allow one of my men accompany him to take the boy safely back home.

"Most certainly, Father. How remiss of me not to think of it."

After an interval of some minutes the wholesome features of the priest re-appeared, glowing from his exertions – his shoulders taut and broad beneath his garb. He had carried the child most of the way, on account of the youngster having twisted his foot during the fall.

My admiration for the man was growing by the hour, and if ever kindly actions spoke louder than kindly words, then *he* was the living embodiment of it. It turned out that only the child's mother had been found at the cabin, and while she had thanked him gratefully by kissing the hem of his robe, she would not be drawn into conversation when she saw the redcoats standing outside.

"These are a strange and peculiar breed of people, Father – how can I help them if they will not speak?"

"I understand your frustration perfectly, Daniel, but remember – they are straining under the yoke of some infernal terror. Give them time – when they find their courage, they will find their voice. I have learnt much myself already, and I will tell you what I can when we have returned from Montpelier tomorrow. It would be pointless of me to share my observations now, until I have had a chance to peruse Buckley's lair. A dice has six sides, Daniel, and at the moment I have only viewed one or two of those faces. By the end of tomorrow I hope to have seen enough of the dice to at least offer you a throw of my theory. At that point we can collate our information – and try to make sense of it all. Can you wait until then?"

"Of course, Father."

"Saunders!" I bellowed.

"Yes, Mr. Parsons?"

"Instruct your men to keep their firelocks at halfcock, with their bayonets fixed and at the ready! Tell them to look sharply!"

Leaving the copse, and gathering ourselves into a tight formation, we proceeded swiftly along the river towards Glenboyne. Mercifully we found our way back to the marketplace without incident, but to our horror (and perhaps some quarter of a mile distant from the village), could be heard the clear appalling cries of baying wolves – many of them. Their howls mingled with the fury of a vicious wind, as we reached the safety of The Eagle Tavern. Although uncertain of the location of the wolves, I now understood for the first time that the threat from these hunters was real, near, and potentially lethal.

I took the opportunity that evening to try and get some much-needed rest, as the injury on my chest was beginning to throb with a dull slow ache. I removed my shirt and examined the wound through the cracked piece of a mirror that stood lopsided on the top of a small dressing table. Gazing into the reflection of this most incongruous of looking glasses, I could see that the skin had been chaffing against the material of my clothing. Where the gash lay across my torso, the muscle and skin had turned a deep purple, with tiny spots of blood around the edges of the cut showing some weeping of the flesh. I began to bathe the chest wound, and overall I was pleased to detect there were no further signs of infection or swelling. But as I pressed gently against the abrasion, a stinging soreness confirmed that the skin was still tender.

How strange can sometimes be the moment when we see our own face. It is never satisfying, frequently disappointing, and occasionally alarming too. I had always prided myself on my personal appearance, with due deference paid to my daily toilet. But before me I saw a dishevelled young man, with his full head of black hair tied back in a pigtail, looking I fancied a touch dusty, and his normally tanned features certainly a shade paler, set off by the large ultramarine blue eyes that seemed now a dull metal grey, and a bruised forehead that added no attraction to a usually smooth brow. Was it I? I'm afraid it was. In my teens I had developed an athletic build through my passion for swimming and horse-riding, and it was my normal habit to maintain a strict regime of exercise. However, I noticed in the glass that I had lost some weight and muscle mass since arriving in Ireland, and this was something of a disappointment to me.

But as I dwelt on these observations, my ears detected a faint rustling coming from outside of my bedroom window. I froze for a moment, not sure if I was imagining it, but again from the alley beside my room, I was certain that I heard a stealthy footfall, very close to the window's edge. My breathing almost stopped when I saw the ragged curtains stir – remembering all too quickly that I had left the casement slightly ajar. I turned from the hand basin terrified lest I make a sound, and reached for my pistol on the stool.

Before I could seize it, a shattering of glass and a fireball of flame burst violently through the curtains as a projectile flashed across the room, exploding against the floor in a myriad of fire tongues. It was a flagon of whiskey set alight with burning rags hanging from its aperture. I stood aghast as the liquid flames engulfed the ground, missing my feet by mere inches. With the instinct of a beast I flung myself upon the bed coverings; and ripping them from the mattress, I dived fearlessly at the blaze, beating the floor beams with the heavy flaxen blankets. I felt the heat singe my hair as I thrashed wildly with my arms and hands to suffocate the combustion.

I had just about extinguished it, when a second missile came hurtling over my shoulder, catching the side of the dressing table, and spewing out its molten contents. I shouted in rage as the room now seemed a veritable inferno, and in desperation more than hope, I lunged at my firearm, seized it with miraculous dexterity, and discharged its contents at the window pane.

The effect was twofold: the assailants withdrew immediately, while a flurry of pounding boots burst forth into the room amid a din of shouts and roars. I threw the water from the hand basin at the dressing table, and seizing the blankets once more, attacked the flames with ferocious energy. Other frantic hands assisted me, and through the smoke my heart rejoiced to see Harry Maguire, his daughter, and Sean Matthews, all moving with lightning speed to quench the fire. In thirty seconds we had it out, and we lay on the floor panting and exhausted. Fr. Moynihan and Corporal Wilkinson appeared all too late on the threshold, amazed at the sight before them.

Incredibly, apart from the stained floor beams and a splintered blackened table, there was remarkably little damage to the room, and the chair where my clothes and satchel lay was completely untouched. I too had made a lucky escape because except for some scorched hair, I had received no skin burns or injury to my person.

"Wilkinson! Get after them! See if you can catch them!"

The tricorne hat was gone in a flash, and Fr. Moynihan helped me to my feet.

"Somebody does not want you here, Daniel," he said with the wryest of smiles.

But the humour was lost on the raging countenance of Harry Maguire.

"I warned you this could happen. Just look at what you've done to my property! I made it clear we wanted no part in this nightmare, and now I find it brought onto my very own doorstep! You said you would protect us – what empty words. How can you defend anyone when you can't watch over the very room you sleep in? I don't care a groat for your investigation. Do you hear? Take your men and get off the premises. I want them gone by tomorrow – otherwise I'll appeal to my local magistrate if I have to."

"I'm sorry, Mr. Maguire, truly I am. I will reimburse you immediately for any damages," I gasped.

"To hell with your money! What good is it if my business is burnt to the ground, and both I and my family end up dead?"

Bridling with affronted indignation, Cathy stepped forward to upbraid him for his choleric remarks.

"Really, Father – how can you be so selfish? It is grossly unfair to blame Mr. Parsons – and talk as though he himself had set the room alight. Have you forgotten that but for his actions this morning little Tilly would now be in a pauper's grave?" retorted Cathy.

The publican stared at her incredulously, his red cheeks bursting with explosive annoyance. For a moment I thought he would strike her, such was his wrath. But unwilling to vent his spleen further, he shot a glare at me, and then a scowl at her, before gathering up his apron and storming out of the room.

"Cathy! What way is that to speak to your father?" protested Sean. "You know he is right. *He* does not care what happens to us… " casting a contemptuous look in my direction. "These English are all the same. They force us to do their bidding, make endless promises, and then leave us to clean up their dirty mess. Come back into the parlour."

"Mr. Parsons will be in need of another place to rest tonight, and this room requires attention. Will you help me re-inforce the window, Sean?" came her firm reply.

His handsome features clouded over with a surly frown, and for the first time I saw a touch of envy in his eyes as he glowered at me. Then shaking his head at her and without replying, he strode haughtily out of the smoke-filled room.

Fr. Moynihan busied himself by picking up the broken pieces of crockery and upending the collapsed table.

"You have not had much luck today, have you, Mr. Parsons?" she remarked. "I will prepare another space for you at the back of the tavern, where I believe there is a vacant room near our storeroom. You should be safe enough there from any intruders."

"Thank you, Miss Cathy."

As she spoke I was struck by the beauty of her large turquoise green eyes, which showed evidence that tears had recently been shed. The blond tresses that adorned her neck perfectly complemented the exquisite whiteness of her skin, a complexion I had noticed to be very common and attractive amongst Irish women. Desperate to avoid my gaze, her eyes fell by accident to glance down at my naked chest, whereupon her two cheeks flushed crimson at the glimpse of my body. Realising I was shirtless I tried quickly to spare her blushes.

"I do beg your pardon, Miss Maguire. Forgive my uncouth appearance. Let me dress myself."

"Your wound I see is bleeding still," she murmured, looking at the injury. "I will fetch you a fresh pitcher of water, a basin of healing salts, and some clean bandages, and will leave them in your care."

"That is most kind of you."

Stealing one last peep at me, she cocked her head, and floated like a vision of loveliness into the dusky hallway.

VIII

MONTPELIER HALL

As a dawn chorus of birds greeted us the next morning, I found myself assembled with Fr. Moynihan, Wilkinson, and a handful of soldiers at the base of the turnpike gate awaiting the arrival of Lundy and his transport. The ardent officer admitted that he had captured no one in the alley the night before, and a search of the neighbouring area revealed no sign of the attackers. To my satisfaction he proudly informed me that he had managed to persuade the local blacksmith to lend us some horses temporarily, despite the farrier's strong protestations and determined efforts not to co-operate. So we agreed amongst ourselves, that Wilkinson and his men would mount these horses, and ride alongside whatever conveyance Buckley would send to take us to his mountain lair.

We did not have long to wait as the same splendid coach from yesterday arrived promptly at the barrier gates, pulled by its four magnificent stallions, with the squat dwarf straining at the reins. Behind it followed a substantial contingent of horsemen, all armed, making up at least twenty riders by my reckoning. Was it Buckley's intention that we should travel in his own private compartment? This would not please the black monk. Nor was I happy that we were entering the same vehicle that almost ran us down the day previous. A worried looking Wilkinson leant forward to me and in muted tones said,

"Beggin' your pardon, Mr. Parsons, and not meanin' to alarm you, but if we must ride broadside with this here gang, it is my duty to point out to you that we will be outnumbered three to one if any dirty business should occur. In the event of an ambush our chances will be poor! And I don't like the look of them, Sir!"

"That is an excellent observation, Corporal, and I commend you for it," I replied softly, "but I do not think their master would be so foolish as to attack the servants of the King's justice. After all, I made it plain to him yesterday that we are here to protect his person, and therefore he has no reason to assault us. Rude, aggressive, and arrogant he may be – but as yet we have no evidence to confirm that Buckley is a threat or even involved in these matters. I suspect this is a show of strength purely – but your point is well taken. Tell your men to prime their muskets, and to keep their scabbards open."

Passing through the turnpike gate we approached the stationary coach. A solemn Lundy opened the door and bade me and Fr. Moynihan enter. It was an invitation I was loath to take, and I wondered if Buckley's cunning was designed to insult us, unnerve us, or put us off entirely? Perhaps all three. My hooded companion wanted to resist, but without our own conveyance I could see no other alternative and reluctantly accepted.

"Me mastuur bids ye welcome Misstuur Parsons, but yer'll need to step lively to it, Sir, as Mastuur Jack has many tings to do terday. Yer'll find comfort and warmt enough inside."

Then lashing the steeds with relish, the diminutive coachman launched the fine vehicle forward with sustained energy, plummeting down the mud-strewn causeway. Thunderous hooves echoed through the air as the coterie of horses, guards, and soldiers followed in its wake. Wilkinson and his men kept pace with the side of the coach, where I could view them through the sash-windows. It was indeed a lavish interior that greeted our eyes, with the lower half of the walls being studded throughout with red satin lining and silver gilt buttons, above which ran a black ebony handrail, that girded the panels to the base of the window sill. Above this on the upper panels were painted some exquisite tableaux of gay rustic scenes, mostly of a bacchanalian nature. Damask cushions rested at our backs, and a black lacquered stool held a silver tray containing two silver goblets and a carafe of wine. A carved ebony roof, embellished with silver garlands of the finest filigree work, completed the stately travelling compartment. The Benedictine looked most uncomfortable in these surroundings, his eyes narrowing under his thickset eyebrows.

"I know this is not ideal, Father, and forgive me for asking you to suffer the indignity of using Buckley's own transport. Believe me, if there was any other way of getting up to Montpelier, I would have taken it gladly. But we are without our own wheels and at a distinct disadvantage."

"There is an unwholesome atmosphere in this space, Daniel, and I do not even wish to hear or speak of the man's name. It is possible that we are now entering his spider's web, and I would not touch anything if I were you, including those refreshments. This is an ungodly receptacle and even to whisper under its roof makes me most nervous."

While saying this, he clasped the strange amulet that hung around his neck and squeezed it tightly between his palms, as I had noticed him do before.

"I hear you clearly, Father, and I will be guided by your advice in these matters. No doubt the master of Montpelier may try to thwart or deceive us at every turn."

"Worse than that, Daniel. If there is any evidence linking him to these deaths he will surely have been busy destroying it. And you witnessed what he thinks of my presence. His disgust will be powerful when he sees me on his land, and he will not make access easy for us. Therefore, I think it is best that you leave me to scout the perimeter of his outhouses with one or two of your men, while you try to enter Montpelier Hall. A few minutes on the hilltop is all I need while you distract him."

"I will try to make it happen," I replied.

The previous night's showers had given way to a brighter day and as we jaunted along the roadside, the splendour of the Wicklow Mountains opened up before us. Pools of dappled sunlight broke through the trees, blending with that invigorating scent of early morning – a heady mixture of moist earth, wet leaves, and nature's plenty. Fresh-faced rabbits sitting at their burrows nibbled delightfully at the dew-drenched grass, whilst a carpet of sun-burst crocuses reflected back the light through a myriad of orange petals. It lifted my spirits to see such beauty.

We soon passed the forlorn cemetery where Nan had been discovered and for half a mile our course stayed level along the broad valley. But further up on this side of the vale the track began to ascend to the base of a much steeper mountain peak, which cast a dark shadow over the lower slopes. Here the terrain became rougher and inhospitable, with large boulders of granite forming jagged lines along the verges of the road, interspersed with dense furrows of silver birch and larch trees. Twisted trunks and splintered branches lay scattered where the recent storm had blasted openings through the pummelled trees. Cascading streams of rainwater penetrated these forest apertures, to fall dramatically down the mountain's side, crossing our path in several places.

At this height it was now possible to look down at some of the surrounding landscape, with the lower mountain slopes partially hidden under a veil of shifting mist. A deep black corrie shimmered below us with small white breakers chasing across its surface, its watery depths making me dizzy to contemplate. The previous abundance of larch and birch trees now gave way to thinner pockets of spruce and mountain ash. Up and up we climbed steadily, and above our heads I could hear Lundy cursing and shouting as the horses struggled with the growing incline.

I noticed that the further we rose the thinner and fresher the air became, with the pervasive scent of resin thrilling through our nostrils from the tree bark around us. The track now altered rather abruptly from a meandering curve, into a more sharply pronounced zig-zag pattern, up the steep sides of what looked like the final climb to the top of this land mass. The horses seemed to recognise their way, whinnying in excitement, and I could only marvel at their trojan strength, as they strained in agony up a seemingly impossible ascent. The path twisted and turned at increasingly dangerous angles for a quarter of a mile, with scree and stones churning under the coach's wheels. I was sure the vehicle must overturn at each of these precipitous bends, but the steeds held fast their course.

After a dozen or more of these hairpin turns, our company finally emerged onto the flat grass summit of Montpelier Hill. The appellation of a hill was certainly misleading as it was located at the crest of the mountain, like some forgotten island at the top of the world. This grassy knoll was of considerable acreage, and was surprisingly level, considering its elevation.

Above us were clear blue skies, and a sharp cool breeze welcomed us from the heavens. I was struck by how difficult it would be for anyone to assault such a location, and it certainly formed a perfect natural barrier against any intruders. Our coach and retinue of riders poured forth onto the green plateau, steam rising from the exhausted animals. Pulling the sash back further my eyes fell upon the extraordinary dwelling that was Montpelier Hall.

Unless you have stood before its edifice it is most difficult to describe the peculiarly striking effect the building has on first seeing it. To begin with – there is its architecture. It is an ugly, powerfully constructed fortress-like building, hewn from crude stonework, designed to withstand the fiercest elements that must lash it daily. It rises several storeys high, except for a central square tower which stands out taller than the main dwelling, containing a large arched window of Gothic design. On either side of this eminence run two wings or galleries of heavily built walls (one on the left and one on the right), each containing mullioned windows, deep set within the brickwork. Above each of these were a series of grotesque and unsettling gargoyles, carved in a similar fashion to the great cathedrals of the continent. The only attempt at artifice was the diamond-paned windows, which gave a certain civilizing effect to an otherwise unwelcoming aspect. The entire building was constructed of large chunks of granite and sandstone, intermingled with mortar of a rough quality, while the roof was formed from a strange admixture of shale and slate.

Its location, too, added to its foreboding facade. Perched as it was upon an open hilltop, it fell victim to an atmosphere of permanent windswept desolation. A snatch of chimneys showed evidence of storm damage, where pots had been ripped from their bases and tiles smashed in the process. Even in the morning sunlight a pervasive gloom shrouded it entirely, and a shadow of unease crept across my heart, knowing that I would soon enter its walls. On either side of Montpelier Hall and forming a small settlement, were a host of barns, stables, and outhouses, each constructed of the same local stonework. Several of these were attached to the main dwelling, forming antechambers, and gave a sprawling effect that made the abode seem much larger than it actually was. Everywhere was a hive of activity, with servants carrying pitchers, stable boys lumbering with harnesses, workmen lifting wood, and farmhands loaded with bails and poultry. Chickens, goats, geese, and a pack of formidable hounds wandered at will, dodging a din of carts, barrels, and pack horses. There was an air of busy industry about the place.

But to my dismay, we were greeted at our arrival by a further grouping of armed riders, including the odious Mick Kearney, Buckley's henchman, who had tried to goad me in the village market. Sitting next to him astride another horse was a man with astoundingly similar features, leading me to believe they must be twin brothers. If possible he was even viler-looking than his sibling double. The main difference between them was a badly healed gash across Mick Kearney's forehead. He leaned forward from his horse to address me inside the coach.

"Good morning, Mr. English, Sir! You're looking a little rough around the edges today. Didn't you sleep very well last night? It looks like the English gentleman didn't sleep too good last night, Pat. Old Maguire's beds aint too comfortable in that tavern, so I'm told."

This jibe resulted in the other brother grinning inanely, displaying a set of rotten yellow teeth. I felt it best to say nothing, but stared coldly at both of them. Wilkinson and his men pulled alongside and made their presence felt, while Lundy wrenched open the door and beckoned us to dismount.

"Mastuur Buckley awaits ye, Misstuur Parsons, if yer'll come dis way. But he's given me stereect orders that he will na have a black monk under his roof. And he's most sure on dat point, Sir – certain sure."

Knowing right well that Fr. Moynihan wished to peruse the hilltop and its outhouses discreetly, I made no attempt to argue this point (insulting though it was), and a glance at the cleric showed his delight at my decision.

"In that case you will allow my men to examine the remains of the burnt carcasses of the wolves, and give them unfettered access to anywhere on this hill. Fr. Moynihan will be under their charge and will go with them – your master need not fear his presence here.

Wilkinson! Dispatch two of your troops to attend to this, and then accompany me with your other men into Montpelier Hall."

"Oh have no fear, Mr. Sir," interrupted Kearney slyly. "We will keep a good eye on your hooded friend. No harm at all will come to him – a personal tour of the estate is what he will get. It is important we should watch over him – God forbid he should stumble into a bog hole – that wouldn't do at all now. Not that there is much to see, you understand?"

"Most thoughtful of you, Mr. Kearney," I replied laconically.

Their small party set off across the grassland, while Lundy turned and marched briskly with the rest of us towards the great Hall. I brought my satchel with me lest there be any challenges to my warrants. The entrance to the building was through a peculiarly reversed L-shaped porch which stood out from the main central tower. Two granite pillars framed the massive doorway, topped by a large stone lintel. Carved into this solid block was the detailed relief of a horned bull, much weathered and covered in lichen. Several of Buckley's militia stood sullenly near the threshold, armed to the teeth. Lundy rapped sonorously on the great oaken door, which opened at a sluggish pace to reveal an old manservant in attendance. In his hand he held up an Irish cruise lamp which flickered unsteadily in the incoming draught, as he scrutinized our faces.

"Ben! Inform Sir Jack will ye, dat Misstuur Parsons has arrived. I will take him to de banqueting parlour to be received dere."

The hunched figure of the aged retainer grunted in reply, making no eye contact with us, and in single file we followed him into the dim interior. I observed that the L-shaped porch had the effect of not allowing anyone to see directly into the building, until the passageway turned left towards a second inner door. For some moments we stood in total darkness until we heard the grating of heavy bolts drawn back, and found ourselves emerging into a large vaulted foyer. It was an impressive and spacious entrance hall with high ceilings of the same distinctive masonry, supported by wide corbelled arches. Suspended from a heavy chain was an imposing black iron chandelier containing dozens of burning candles. The pungent smell of the tallow and dry musty atmosphere combined to form a shortness of air throughout. Directly ahead was a grand staircase of smooth granite blocks, which led up through the building's central tower. Lundy beckoned us to follow him and we ascended two flights to the first floor. Turning right, he brought us into a fine-looking chamber furnished with the accoutrements of a discerning gentlemen.

The floor was of polished oak and covered by a single rectangular rug of capacious dimensions. Across it, and running the length of the room, was a long ebony dining table exquisitely carved, surrounded by at least twenty high-backed chairs. Great tapestries, filled with hunting scenes and nymphs bathing in Greek temples, lined the walls. On the table was a splendid array of pewter jugs, tureens, goblets, and ornamental plates, interspersed with silver candlesticks. A roaring hearth of burning logs filled the south-facing wall, with arched alcoves on either side containing benches where one could sit close to the fire. High above this and adorning the wall was a triangular black shield bearing the Buckley coat of arms. It was a simple motif – of three bull's heads, all white, two resting on the upper half of the shield, and one resting on the lower half, divided by a white line. In front of the fire and stretched out across the fender, was a magnificent Irish wolfhound licking its paws in easeful pleasure. Old Ben vanished through an ante-chamber doorway, and moments later we heard the approach of a much sturdier footfall. The door was flung open and once more I beheld that man whose presence caused me great unease.

"Lundy! You are late again! What took you so damn long getting here?"

"Beggin' yer pardon mastuur... but de horses were strainin' sometin' fierce comin' up dat hill... an well it was..."

"Straining did you say? I'll stretch your bloody neck from the end of a rope the next time you keep me waiting. And then you will hang as hog meat for the hounds! You wretched little..."

He was about to land a blow of his fist across the

dwarf's face, when on seeing the room was not empty he checked his impulse.

"Ah! We have some esteemed company, do we not? Welcome, Mr. Parsons, to Montpelier Hall! I trust you and your men had a pleasant journey and did not find the terrain too taxing? Excuse the stupidity of my valets – they are a rum lot at the best of times, and ignorant boors at the worst."

He strode across the rug and took up a position beside the fireplace, resting his hand upon the mantelpiece. Hanging from his shoulders was a finely woven banyan, a comfortable garment similar to a dressing gown, and much favoured by the Irish aristocracy. I had seen it bedeck many fashionable gentlemen in the parlours of Dublin, and marvelled at its elegant design. Buckley's was made of silk damask, and matched his ribbed silk breeches. Then stretching himself up to his full height, he eyed me with an intimidating glare.

"Time is of the essence, Mr. Parsons, and you could not have picked a busier week for your enquiries. So I am sure you will understand that this must be a brief interview. Now what is it exactly that I can do for you, and what is it that you hope to achieve at Montpelier?"

His white eye disturbed me greatly, but not half so much as that iniquitous blue eye which seemed to pierce through heart and soul. I thought carefully before answering him, as to how to make it seem justified that a search of his outhouses would be necessary. It was essential to grant Fr. Moynihan the requisite few minutes he needed – and I would dissemble if I had to.

"Well, Sir Buckley, my chief concern is for your own safety and indeed the protection of the good people of Glenboyne. Your theory that these recent attacks are the work of wolves has great merit, and my men would like to examine whatever is left of them on your premises – in case any trace of human bones survived your flames. Because if I could establish that they were the cause of these dreadful deaths – it would be such a relief to the community, and I could report this with confidence to Dublin Castle. You would not mind if they sift through the debris?"

"If it makes you comfortable, Mr. Parsons, by all means search through what you will. But Mick and Pat will already have cleared away most of the remnants from the bonfires, and I cannot imagine you will find much amongst the ashes. Your concern for my safety is most touching – but my boys are well equipped here to protect my personage. Your visit I fear will be a fruitless one."

"And if it is not wolves, Sir Buckley? What then? The attacker or attackers unknown could be assassins? Or worse? You must surely have heard the rumours in Glenboyne?"

My pulse quickened as I gathered my courage.

"Rumours? What rumours?" he snapped, with an

upraised brow.

"Of a creature. The locals are claiming they have seen and heard some devilish monster that has terrorised the vales and woods hereabouts. They clearly feel there is a connection between this thing and the massacres of recent weeks, and live in dread of its presence. Fantastical? Yes I know. But I myself and my men saw and heard something uncanny as we entered Kelly's Gorge."

Buckley scrutinized me momentarily, but then threw his head back and proceeded to laugh in a very forced fashion.

"Do you expect me to believe that you have come all this was way to hunt for spooks and goblins? What you speak of is nothing more than the idle gossip of wagging tongues, the tittle and tattle of ignorant peasants. Yes – some of this nonsense has reached my ears. Your Irish farmer is a superstitious fool, Mr. Parsons – ever content to blame his woes on fairies and pookas. To listen to them in the village would make a man hoarse with laughter. I am astonished that you would give credence to such chatter."

"And yet, Sir Buckley – whatever we encountered in that gorge was strong enough to haul away one of my men. Not a trace of him was left and our horses were maddened with fear! We all heard its strange call – and it was a sound like nothing I know of."

"Wolves I tell you!" he expostulated. "They can carry off anything – even a horse. Have you not heard a wolf pack in the frenzy of an attack? There is nothing more terrifying, Mr. Parsons, I can assure you – and their shrieks would freeze a man's blood to ice. I cannot count how much livestock I have lost to them these last two winters. Besides - how do you know it was not thieves, or Jacobite rebels who took your man? The country is awash with traitors to the crown and they would do much worse than hang a redcoat! They would tear him limb from limb until there was nothing left but his bones. Do not underestimate the savagery of these people."

"Perhaps, Sir Buckley! Perhaps! But why would Jacobite rebels wish to murder innocent women? They surely could not give cause to merit such barbaric slaughter. I am told those ladies were much respected in Glenboyne, innocent souls barely grown to womanhood."

Buckley stroked the wolfhound irritably.

"Really, Mr. Parsons! What makes you think that I could possibly know the answers to such questions? I am not a sage, Sir – nor an oracle seer. And I do not presume to understand the nature of these killings – I can only tell you what I think has happened. Nothing more."

I did not believe a word he said – despite the strength of his insistence. Deep inside, my thoughts were turning to The Hellfire Club, and I felt my conscience goading me to broach the subject with him. I knew it was madness to think of doing so – likely dangerous. Even its name sent a shiver down my spine, and I wondered what Fr. Moynihan would advise me if he could hear my thoughts? I felt sure he would stay my hand – so I held back from further questioning. Buckley's steely gaze seemed almost to sense my apprehension, and a slight tremor came over me as my imagination told me he could read my mind.

"Is there anything else?" he inquired, with a face of stone.

"No, Sir Buckley – you have been most helpful," I lied.

"Good! Well, Sir... after you have concluded your perambulations on the hill with your men, Lundy will take you back to Glenboyne. If I can be of any further assistance, don't hesitate to contact me. I am frequently in the village on private business, and I feel certain our paths will cross again – soon. Lundy! Attend to your duties!"

The dwarf bowed in response, and led us once more down the stairs, through the porch, and out onto the bustling hilltop, where Buckley's workers continued apace with their daily chores. There I found the black monk already waiting for us (with the soldiers in tow), displaying a strained look on his face, but managing to retain all the while a perfect self-composure. The Kearney brothers were not far behind him, their muskets still bristling in the morning sun and pointing in a menacing fashion. We did not linger – we did not speak – and Wilkinson quickly re-formed his mounted bodyguard as we left Montpelier's domain. Before noon we found ourselves back at the turnpike gate, with McIntyre the gatekeeper still demanding ten pence for the pleasure of his service and his choleric outbursts.

IX

A POUCH WITH A DRAWSTRING

"Over here!"

"Why so secretive?"

"Because what I have to tell and show you must be for our eyes and ears only!"

It was late that same afternoon, and Fr. Moynihan had brought me to an abandoned well in the middle of a grove of yew trees growing in a field at the back of the Eagle Tavern. We were standing next to the dilapidated wheel and pulley, and the cleric looked more serious than I had ever seen him before. Although less than ten minutes separated us from the inn, we stood alone in total solitude, as the Corkman had insisted on.

"You are ready to speak of what you have learned?" I suggested.

"Yes, Daniel – you have been most patient with me. And I dared not say anything until we had left Montpelier Hill and its prying servants. I have not yet seen all six sides of the dice, but I have certainly learnt enough to confer with you. Now watch!"

So saying, he removed from his habit a small white cloth which he placed carefully on the earth, and then from the pocket of his robe he withdrew a pouch of a deep purple hue, tied at the top with a white drawstring. Turning it upside down and untying the string, he proceeded to empty the contents of the bag onto the cloth, displaying a set of the most extraordinarily carved small pieces of oblong wood, almost egg-shaped – each about two and a half inches in length, and all marked with peculiar dark symbols of a cryptic nature.

"Good heavens!" I exclaimed. "What in the world are they?"

"Runes," he said solemnly.

"Runes?"

"Runes," he repeated.

There was a long pause, with the only noise a sigh of wind in the boughs above us.

"Wait a minute... but I remember now... yes... I had an old school teacher in Cheshire who told us briefly about them. Aren't they something to do with folklore and witchcraft? I even remember him mentioning about curses and magic spells! Could that be right? They are odd-looking – what are they made of? Can I see?"

I leant forward to touch one, but just in time my robed companion slapped my hand away.

"Be careful! If you are in any way superstitious it would be wiser not to handle them. You had a most remarkable tutor – as there are few teachers anywhere who even remember the existence of runes, and fewer still who would dare to mention such things."

"But what are they, Father? And where did you get them from?"

"The latter is easily explained, the former more complicated. When we came across the overturned chaise and Geoffrey Harold lying in the rain, I found the first one in the mud lying next to his body where it had fallen from his hand. The second I discovered at the cemetery, still gripped in the palm of Nan Harold's corpse. A third I noticed on the ground in the outhouse of our friend the surgeon. And several more I unearthed in the grass near the bonfires on Montpelier Hill."

"I see. And now that you point it out to me, I do recollect clearly watching you pick up something from the muck before we got his body into the coach. Now too I understand your intense scrutiny of Nan's body in the graveyard – you were looking for these objects. To find them at all in the doctor's outhouse and amongst the weeds of Montpelier – is quite an achievement. You have a sharp eye, Fr. Moynihan! But what in God's name is their purpose? A sinister one, no doubt?"

The Benedictine looked cautiously over his shoulder, and walked in a circle around the well, until he had searched any likely places close by where an eavesdropper could be hiding. Satisfied we were alone – he returned to me.

"You can be sure of it, boy!" came his reply. "In this case certainly. The use of runes in Ireland goes back to ancient times, long before Christianity reached these shores, when it is said that druids and shamans used them to cast magic spells or curses on those they gave them to. Legend has it that the runes could be used for good or evil. They are carved from the wood of the yew tree, and the strange characters you see on them are a form of runic language, designed to cast the spell. These black symbols are burnt into the wood using charcoal. Then in order for the spell to work it is said that the rune must be handed directly into the palm of its intended victim. Only then can the sorcery take effect."

"Are you telling me that these pieces of etched wood are the instrument of some diabolical magic which killed all these people?" I exclaimed.

"No, Daniel. I am not advocating something so simple. Personally, I do not believe in superstition or in the supposed power of any witchcraft. Yes, I believe in evil and its agents, but far too often the black arts are used as a decoy to hide a cunning murderer. I am simply explaining to you the historical use of runes in days gone by, and the power they had to terrify people. Clearly, whoever gave these runes to those unfortunate victims may themselves have believed in their powers, or they may have used them to try to literally frighten the life out of their selected prey, by threatening them with immediate death. I am convinced that fear was a key element in the equation – the runes were designed in this instance to signal to the receiver by means of terror, that they soon would die."

"But how can you be so sure that these runes warned of destruction?" I continued, fascinated with his detailed revelations.

I waited for his response.

In answer the monk leant forward, and using a white glove on his hand, he picked up one of the wooden pieces. Holding it up to view between his forefinger and thumb, he said, "Because of this symbol!"

I examined the rune and made out a small black marking on the pale wood, which if it had been written with a quill would look something like this;

ᛇ

"What does it mean?" I implored.

"Death," came the terrible answer, "it is the runic symbol of EIHWAZ, meaning certain death by violent means."

"Good God! I understand now. But this thing, the terror that we heard in the trees! You are not going to tell me that the runes conjured up some kind of demon or devil to slaughter these people?"

"As I said, I do not hold with superstitious beliefs, nor do I give credence to sorcery or magic. However I will admit, that like Wilkinson I noticed the hoof marks leading to the brook that night in the gorge, their indentations all around the toppled vehicle. Something made them – and I spotted the same broad markings on the ground below Nan's body in the graveyard. These facts cannot be ignored, and they leave us with a serious mystery. What caused them? And what are we dealing with? I do not know the answers yet – but I am inclined to put my trust in logic and common sense. If you have enemies, Daniel, or a group of people you wish to remove, what better device to get rid of them (in a deeply superstitious people) than to have it put abroad that a monster is afoot, or that the Devil himself is wreaking revenge upon their community! Why, then you can kill as many as you like with impunity. After all, if the Devil is responsible – who else can be blamed?"

"You speak as if you did not believe in the Devil, Father?" I quipped.

"Oh I do, Daniel. I do. The Evil One is alive and well, and has many servants throughout the world. But why would he come to a village in Wicklow to kill a few women? That does not make sense. But we can be certain of several things. Yes – runes have been used to terrorize, or possibly induce death through fear. Yes – these runes are evidence that some form of Satanism or the occult is being practised in this matter. Yes – there is something, someone, or persons unknown out there attacking these people. Yes – more blood will be shed, and more bodies will be found if we cannot find the attacker or assailants soon. Yes – we are dealing with a vicious, ruthless, and sadistic killer or killers. And yes, I firmly believe that Jack Buckley and a resurgent Hellfire Club have something to do with it."

"What makes you so certain that this club even exists?"

"Because, several days before we left Dublin, I had seen another small article in The Dublin Weekly Journal, which alluded to a rumour that this wayward club had recently been re-instated by the Right Honourable Sir Jack Buckley of Montpelier Hall, despite complaints from other members of the aristocracy to have it disbanded on the grounds of immorality. The newspaper was short on facts, but it made reference to stories that this secret society was complicit in drunkenness, debauchery, lewd acts, and possibly the practice of the black arts. I thought, this could be an exaggeration, but now I see considerable significance in these claims."

"That ties in with reports we received in Dublin Castle too," I remarked, "but information is very scarce on this group's activities. We could find out virtually nothing about it!"

"Not surprising," the cleric replied. "And while you were inside Montpelier Hall, I discovered some other disturbing facts. Everywhere on the hilltop were signs of copious bonfires, some enormous by the size of the burn marks, which closely resembled the great ritualistic fires of the heathens of old. At the rear of the outhouses I noticed a dilapidated charnel house, and requesting that I needed to relieve myself urgently, your soldiers made sure that I got inside, where I could have some privacy. Those thugs the Kearney brothers did their best to frustrate my entrance to it – but the redcoats blocked their way. Once there I found mounds of charred bones piled high nearest the doorway. I could see that rushed attempts had been made to incinerate them in a large furnace. I must have counted dozens of jaw bones, mainly of cattle – much more than could be accounted for by a handful of wolf attacks! And in the ashes, almost obliterated, was the burnt remains of a spirit drum, a musical instrument used in ceremonies of the occult, with a part of the drum skin still showing a decipherable runic symbol, which the flames had not engulfed. All this I saw in seconds, and it certainly smelt of satanic ritual slaughter. Having let nature take its course I emerged from the structure apologising profusely to the Kearney brothers for my weak bladder, and thanked them for their patience. They were both in a vile fury, and surely would have murdered me, but for the protection of your men.

Finally, as we returned across the hilltop I had to fake a fall to the ground, pretending I had tripped, which gave me some crucial seconds to pocket a rune that I had spotted earlier amongst one of the grass hummocks. A monk's robe can be most useful in ground coverage!"

"So we have our man! We can arrest him now! Yes?"

"Not yet, Daniel. There are still several sides of the dice to be revealed. Buckley could claim that the runes were planted there by others, or that the cattle were diseased, starved, or killed by wolves, and had to be burned. He could even say the spirit drum was not his – perhaps given him as a gift from friends travelling abroad. He could make any number of excuses."

"And he also has privileges as an aristocrat and member of the Irish ascendency," I pointed out.

"Yes. I'm afraid you will have to catch him in the act, or find a corpse or victim on his premises. But I repeat, I am now personally convinced that he is involved in the practice of the occult, that he is behind these runes, that The Hellfire Club is alive and well, and that he is involved in these deaths. I counted, too, at least thirty armed men at Buckley's disposal. You are outnumbered and cannot take him by force, until you receive re-enforcements. I doubt he will let us up there again without a fight."

A POUCH WITH A DRAWSTRING

He gathered up the white cloth with the runes (making sure, I noticed, not to touch them, by using his gloves) and replaced them in the purple pouch.

"Well done, Father. The light is already fading and that dark cloud threatens a downpour – so let us return to the tavern without delay. We are making steady progress."

X

TWO COCKED HAMMERS

More cunning than a fox is your Irish rain cloud – ever ready to sting that unsuspecting traveller with a lash of its fearsome tail. Just when you think it has passed you by, it unloads a deluge, a calculated insult of rainwater, dropped it seems almost out of spite. So it was now, as we ran back across the field, onto the nearest track, pounded by the heavy droplets. The chimneys of the inn could be seen in the distance peeping out above a cluster of trees, but we had several lanes and some grassland to negotiate before reaching it.

Gaining the top of the track we sprinted onto the main pathway, where a small patch of woodland overhanging it cast many shadows. And there, to our astonishment, we saw two figures, one lying on the ground, and a second kneeling on the earth trying to assist the first to get up. Beside them was an agitated horse, shaking its mane and whinnying nervously, its reins trailing on the mud. I instantly recognised the gracious outline of Cathy Maguire hunched over the athletic form of Sean Matthews. We raced to their sides, anxious at what we may find.

"Miss Cathy! Are you in trouble? What happened?" I panted. Instinctively, I helped her lift Sean to his feet before she could answer, while Fr. Moynihan tried to steady the nervous mare.

"Oh, Mr. Parsons – it is you, thank God. We were coming back from the blacksmith when something unnerved the horse and made it rear, throwing us both to the ground. I have taken many falls over the years and managed to sustain this one, but Sean I fear has hurt himself."

"I'm fine. There is no need for you to worry," came the youth's reply, as he stood erect and rubbed himself down, apparently uninjured. He wrenched himself away from my supporting shoulder, as though disgusted I should aid him, and glared at me all the while.

"And what about you, my own brave girl?" he said tenderly. "I was worried sick you would break your neck. Let me have a look at you. Not a mark, it seems – you are a lucky girl, Cathy Maguire."

He caressed her affectionately, tracing back those curls to examine her for any bruises, and then kissed her passionately, full upon the lips.

"But your foot," he remarked, "are you limping slightly? You don't seem to be standing properly. Can you walk, love?"

"Now don't fuss, Sean. I may have twisted it slightly – that's all. I will be as right as rain in no time."

"You mean you will be drenched by the rain in no time, if we don't get out of it soon," he grinned, hugging her tightly. His words were indeed prophetic as the cloudburst pelted us from above, showing no signs of slackening off.

"Mr. Matthews is right, Miss Cathy. It would be best if you got home at all speed before you catch a chill," I interjected. "We were just on our way back to the tavern ourselves, when we spotted your predicament. Can you remount the horse with your sore foot?"

"I feel sure I can," she replied. "Thank you once again, Mr. Parsons, for your kindness in helping us. It is most gentlemanly of you. And you too, Father – the steed would undoubtedly have bolted but for your firm hand. Sean – help me up, will you?"

I was about to offer them my assistance, when a sound drew my attention to the thick undergrowth beneath the heavy mass of trees behind us. For a hundred feet or more this copse enshrouded the pathway where we stood, before clearing out onto a stretch of open grazing land ahead of us, that led to the back yard of the inn. I swung around, and through the dismal haze of rainwater I scanned the boughs for any sign of movement. I was shocked to realize that it was already almost dark, making it difficult to define anything.

A steady breeze was playing amongst the foliage, causing the branches to creak and moan. But above the wind I could hear a clear crunching sound of heavy footfalls, and the snapping of crushed deadwood. Something was approaching through the trees. My heart began to pound. Then to my horror, beginning slowly at first, I heard that same diabolical hissing sound which had frozen our blood some nights previously, rising out of the murky shadows, its baleful tones filling the air. The mare began to plunge and jerk violently as the black monk struggled to control it. I wrenched myself from my craven stupor, and hurled myself into action.

"Sean! Cathy! Get on that horse and ride for your lives. Get out of here! Do you hear me? Father! Go with them. You will have to run for it. I will try to hold it off. Move! All of you!"

The young couple seemed paralysed with terror, but the cleric thrust them onto the beast with lightning agility, and had them firmly mounted in an instant. Before they could reproach me, I gave a whack to the horse's haunches and sent it at a ferocious gallop through the mud and rain. The priest stared at me incredulously, half in rage and half in stupefaction.

"What are you doing, Daniel? Are you mad? You cannot hope to stop it alone!"

"There is no time to argue, Father. Whatever it is, I can delay it a few seconds to give you and the others a head start. Trust me, I beg of you, and for the love of Christ – run! Run until your heart bursts!"

A lifetime of wisdom told him I was right, and gathering up his garments he bolted forward with impressive determination, never once looking backwards. I turned to face my unknown assailant, and withdrew two pistols from my jacket that I had placed there earlier. The night before, I had made sure to load the weapons with my powder keg, and had both pans primed and charged. I cocked back the two hammers and waited. It was essential that I discharge them at precisely the right moment to have a fighting chance of escape.

That appalling sound came ever closer, and as my eyes became accustomed to the dark, I could make out a fierce tumult of agitated leaves and brittle branches being snapped asunder. A tall black silhouette began to emerge, displaying a stilted jerky motion to its steps, which gave me the impression of something broad and powerful. Seeing its location I now became possessed of an insatiable rage to confront it. This too, I think, was born of the dread of my dire situation. In consternation I raised the first pistol and screamed out loud.

"DAMN YOU TO HELL! Devil or beast, you will taste my shot!"

I squeezed the trigger, the hammer sparked, and the barrel exploded with a deafening blast. The bullet flashed through the air catching my enemy broadside, ripping into the thick brambles. Had I hit it? Surely not? And yet the explosion seemed to have the desired effect, as my attacker faltered slightly behind the leaves, as though taken by surprise. But then began a stentorian roar, a sickening howl that augured dreadful violence, and its dark bulk began to move again. Sweat trickled down my palm as I raised the second firearm aloft, my arm shaking tremulously. A huge limb, like the top half of a thigh, began to push through the foliage, and I pulled the trigger with all my resolve.

A thunderous boom issued from the barrel, louder than the first, and the pellet shot through the thicket with stunning force. I heard a ricochet as the metal projectile struck something hard with a glancing blow, and the thing seemed to reel hard to one side, letting out an audible wheezy grunt. It had stopped dead in its tracks, and I realised that here was my opportunity. At school I had outpaced most of my fellow students at running, and my agility as a swimmer had taught me strength and stamina. I had calculated that a two-minute sprint could be enough to reach the back gate of the tavern yard, if I could outrun the danger behind me. And so I dashed like a madman, tearing along the track in giant strides, my feet pounding through the soft wet earth. The rain continued to mar my vision, but I shot forward with manic energy, my legs pulsating vigorously. I had just cleared the trees onto the open grass, when I heard that eerie shriek once more behind me, and this time a heavy tread was in close pursuit. I could not mistake it.

A panic now seized me, and I re-doubled my efforts, gritting my teeth vehemently. Up ahead I could see the distant powerful figure of Fr. Moynihan racing tirelessly towards the inn, and I used him as a marker. My legs I knew would carry me – but my breathing could cost everything if not controlled. I swallowed an intake of air, and with herculean forcefulness I projected myself forward at an even greater speed. The footfalls continued to pursue me, but I dared not look back, as any hesitation could cost me my life. The hissing slacked off slightly as I put some distance between me and my pursuer, and this gave a renewed courage and energy to my purpose. On I bounded, the blood coursing through my veins, my calves aching from their exertions.

I could see the walls of the tavern, perhaps some hundred yards distant, and several blurred forms moving near the gates and shouting at me. But the distance and the rain had made it hard to hear them. I was half-way across the field by now, when, through the corner of my eye I began to detect that something else was racing towards me, from the left side of the meadow. Was this the ravings of an overheated brain? A series of high-pitched howls proved that I was not imagining it, as I saw several white forms with glinting eyes, making fast in my direction. It was wolves – three or four at least. Maybe more.

Great God! What sinister bad luck was this? But a will to live consumed me, and I hurtled myself onwards towards my sanctuary. Closer and closer the gates loomed, until to my delight I could see Wilkinson and several redcoats waving frantically at me, some rushing forward to my aid, and each echoing the same refrain.

"GET DOWN! GET DOWN!"

I ducked as a volley of shots tore across my head, finding their targets with lethal accuracy, as several of the wolves whimpered and slumped to their deaths. One lupine brute, although injured, continued to pursue me doggedly, snapping and snarling, its hot breath almost on my shins. I made a last dash for the gate, and just in time saw Wilkinson plunge his bayonet into the beast, impaling it, as it tried to leap forward onto my back. A crackling of muskets continued to fire randomly as the remaining wolves scattered into the night shadows. The hissing presence had also vanished, and nothing of it could be seen in the darkness. I collapsed through the barriers, gasping in a heap on the gravel yard.

"Seal the entrance fast! Get those gates closed!" roared the corporal.

"And use carts, barrels, or anything you can find to push up against them."

Half a dozen hands obeyed his order, and the doors slammed tightly shut. A broken cart was turned on its side and pressed against the beams, whilst large planks of wood were placed at angles to stop the hinges from budging.

Fr. Moynihan was kneeling close beside me, bent forward and holding his sides, panting furiously. He turned to look at me, and a twinkle in his eye confirmed his relief at seeing me. Neither of us could utter a word as we struggled to regain our breathing. It was a full minute before I could clear my throat and find strength to speak.

"The next time you wish to tell me something privately, or in total solitude, kindly do so indoors, Father, and not in the middle of a field – is that clear?"

He stared sternly at me momentarily, and I gave back as much in return. But his expression changed quickly to a smile, and that smile to a cheeky grin, and that grin to a tiny chuckle, and that chuckle to a pronounced laugh, until his whole chest was heaving with that bell-like resonance, which boomed from those airy lungs of his. Whether it was the sheer joy of being alive – or a nervous thrill at escaping death, I too began to laugh, slowly at first, and then more loudly, as the priest's exuberance melted away the years of my reserve. Before we both knew it we were breathless once again, but this time for a more amiable reason. We had earned the right to do so I felt, and I was not ashamed for either of us.

XI

DISCORDANT VOCALS

"Wilkinson! You are a courageous soul, and I owe you my life."

I had just devoured a breakfast of bacon, cabbage, and barley cakes, and was sitting in the alcove near the tavern fire the next morning. The stalwart soldier blushed slightly at my unexpected compliment and smiled broadly from ear to ear in appreciation.

"Thank God you made it, Sir! It was a close call by all accounts."

"Too close!" I replied. "And but for you I would surely have been ripped asunder. I doubt too if my intrepid friend would have made it back without your quick thinking, and the excellent marksmanship of your soldiers. Did the young pair make it safely to the inn?"

"Yes, Sir! They were well ahead of you, and the horse got them here quickly. And I have other good news. One of my riders succeeded in getting through to Rathfarnham Castle and alerted Colonel Butler to our situation. He discovered a forgotten track over the mountain peaks that took him around the side of Kelly's Gorge, although it damn near killed him and his horse, so rough was the ground. But he did it, and could inform me that a detachment of soldiers and engineers had left the Castle to clear the mudslide with all possible speed. It is expected that the pass could be open in two, or three more days at the latest. A company of men will then be despatched to Glenboyne to assist us as you requested. Harkin too can confirm that the coach has finally been repaired."

"Excellent! You are indeed the bringer of good tidings. Where is Harkin now?"

"Down at the local blacksmiths, Sir, collecting the vehicle."

"When he returns gather up a handful of your men, and get Harkin to transport you back to Kelly's Gorge this morning. Do a thorough search again for Private Taylor. I cannot bear to think of his body dumped somewhere in that hollow, denied even a Christian burial. It is forlorn, I know, to think that he is still alive, but until his body is found there is still some hope. Stay in tight formation and do not let your men stray. And get out of there long before sunset. Leave the borrowed horses and the other redcoats here. I will have need of them. Understand?"

"Yes, Mr. Parsons!"

"Where is Fr. Moynihan this morning?"

"Still asleep, Sir!"

"Mmmm...hardly surprising. Leave him there. He must be exhausted and has earned his rest. We will not disturb him until this afternoon. Leave Private Saunders with me also – as he has proved himself most reliable."

The sprightly corporal went off about his business, his tricorne hat bobbing proudly on his head. It was still early and the inn was quiet with no customers in sight. I finished the barley cakes and washed them down with a flagon of mead. Perhaps it was the full belly or the potency of the drink, combined with yesterday's physical endeavours, but I felt a heavy lethargy descend suddenly upon me; as I slumped forward onto the table, and fell into a welcome doze. However, my half-dreams were not at all pleasant, as my mind swirled with a panoply of runic symbols flashing like great fire-brands above the leaping flames of a large bonfire. I could feel the heat searing my skin, and wanted to move, but couldn't. Chanting could be heard as blurred figures in strange attire held something high above their heads. Standing on a podium, his sword raised upwards, was the striking figure of Jack Buckley, his eyes staring lasciviously at mine. I was bound hand and foot. Two familiar voices began to sneer close by, as the grotesque features of the Kearney brothers came into view, each grabbing me by the arm. They punched and kicked my body while lifting me ever closer to that growing blaze. Their insults clamoured in my ears and I tried to give vent to a scream, but nothing issued from my lips. I shook my head in violent frenzy as I tried to free the chords, but found my head pressed against something flat and hard.

I opened my eyes and saw the empty tankard I had drunk from, my cheeks covered in perspiration, with my face lying downwards on the tavern table. I gasped a sigh of relief that it was but a nightmare, and yet I could swear those voices were still hard by! I raised and shook my head, and found I had not moved from the alcove near the hearth of the inn. How long my slumber lasted I could not tell, but the voices were real enough, as I made out the discordant vocals of Mick and Pat Kearney in conversation with Cathy Maguire at the bar. The recess where I sat was at right angles to where they stood and in deep shadow, so that if I did not move too rashly I could remain undiscovered, and perhaps learn something. Leaning forward a mere inch I was able to cock my eye around the corner, and saw Mick Kearney slouching heavily across the bar, his fingers rapping on the counter. His brother was busy downing some ale.

"Where is the rent?" snapped the scarred forehead, "and what delays that old fool your father? Sent you out to make excuses has he? Master Jack is tired of waiting, do you hear? You owe him four weeks and he has been extra generous in allowing you time to get it. But he is running out of patience fast."

"My father is doing his best, Mr. Kearney – I know

he will have it for you very soon," she pleaded. "But the people have no money – they barely have enough to eat, and some are even starving! The casks of ale cannot be sold in these desperate times, and so few travellers are staying in Glenboyne. What are we to do? Please grant us another week – oh spare us some mercy! You cannot imagine how hard it is!"

"MERCY? Pah!" he snarled. "And you cannot imagine Sir Buckley's rage if I go out that door without your money! He is waiting outside you know, and he may not be as understanding as I am. I have no intention of feeling his wrath across my back on your account, my dear. Do you get it? Now pay up – or Pat here might just get a case of the fidgets. Isn't that right, Pat? Oh Lord, when he gets those fidgets – he becomes awful restless, you know. Starts to drop things like – knocks stuff over. It would be shockin' if he accidently broke anything, and you having such a tidy tavern and all."

Pat Kearney giggled like an obsequious ass.

"We can give you one week's rent now, and the rest next weekend," persisted Cathy, pushing the money into his palm. "It is as much as we can offer. I promise we will have it all by then. Have a heart, Mr. Kearney. My father is a good man and will honour his word."

Kearney chewed his gums and spat on the floor.

"Well maybe... just maybe... if you can't pay it all today. There are other ways to pay a debt, you know?

I could take a weeks rent now, and perhaps... well... er... a clever girl like you knows what I mean?"

His salacious eyes travelled all over her nubile figure, and bending forward he grabbed her by the wrist, his decrepit brother cheering him on.

I knocked over my tankard deliberately, sending it crashing to the ground, and kicked the table out in front of me. I thrust my hand within my pocket, extended my forefinger, and pretended that I had a pistol. Kearney swung around violently, upending a stool, while toppling a tray of plates onto the floor. His bearded face bristled with intense fury, as the purple scar upon his brow protruded angrily. Luckily, his musket was leaning against the nearest bench, just inches out of reach, where he eyed it most jealously.

"I would not do that if I were you," I warned. "Take your hands off Miss Maguire and back away."

"Why, Mr English – what a regular jack rabbit you are! Popping up here, there, and everywhere! We have a way of dealing with nuisance rabbits up on Montpelier. What do you mean sneaking around back there and listening in on our business? And I have not touched the sweet lady at all. This is rent day in Glenboyne, and it is none of your concern what we are up to."

"You are a liar, Kearney! Rent or no rent, you will treat Miss Maguire with respect. And you will not harass, bully, or manhandle her. To do so is an offense, and the next time I catch you breaking the law I will have you arrested, bound in chains, and taken back to Dublin. I suggest you accept what she can offer, and come back for the remainder next week. You will also address me as, Sir, and nothing else."

"Take me back in chains, will ye? Aren't you over-stepping the mark just a little bit, Mr? There wasn't any manhandling of any sort, and as for threats - well, the only person I see pointing a pistol at anyone is you! Aiming at me with a loaded firearm – I would say that is breaking the law. So you and who's army is going to take me to Dublin, Mr. lawmaker?"

He lunged to grab his weapon, and as he turned around to point it at me, a firm voice from behind the counter yelled at him.

"THIS ARMY!"

It was Saunders, who had pushed through the ragged cloth that acted as an entrance between the bar and the private rooms – his firelock poised at Kearney's head. Behind him was another redcoat, with Harry Maguire and Sean Matthews close in tow.

"KEARNEY! You insatiable fool! Drop it! Or by God I will break this cane across your wretched back!"

This ejaculation came from the opposite direction of the floor, through the main tavern doors, which were thrust open by the silver-toped cane of Jack Buckley. His felt-brimmed hat and towering figure filled the threshold, whereupon he strode angrily across the floor, followed by several armed servants. His black satin coat, and 'boot cuff' sleeves shimmered brightly, where the early morning sun reflected back the gold twist and fine embroidery. A dazed Mick Kearney, unsure of what to do, stood helpless and gaping, as his master closed to within a foot of him. The thug moved to speak, but before he could open his mouth Buckley brought his cane down viciously across his arms, knocking the heavy weapon out of his grip, where it clattered to the ground.

"IDIOT!" I ought to break your bloody neck! I told you there was to be no trouble. Get out! The two of you!"

"But master... she wouldn't... " he protested.

"GET OUT! And take that musket with you," roared Buckley.

Mick Kearney's eyes now glowered with murderous thoughts, but he and his twin sibling slumped out of the building like two beaten curs.

"And you, Sir!" rasped Buckley, as he approached me. "Tell that soldier to stand his weapon down. How dare he threaten me and my workers on our rent collection round. What is the meaning of this outrage?"

"It is fine, Saunders! Lower your musket!" I ordered.

"This is a public tavern, Sir", he bellowed, "where I or my agents can visit freely, especially to collect what is rightfully mine. If I wish to drink, or revel here I will do so, and if I wish to eat here – I will do that too, and neither you nor your cohorts from Dublin will stop me. I showed you hospitality yesterday, and not content with disrupting my affairs at Montpelier, or insulting me by distracting me so that your Benedictine spy could rummage through my sheds – oh yes, I know all about that, Sir! – you now attempt to interfere in my legitimate business, by stopping the collection of my rents!"

"He was attempting to intimidate Miss Maguire using force," I argued.

"Lies, Sir! Lies!" he fumed, working himself up to ever greater indignation as he stood before me. "It is YOU who has a pistol pointing straight at me in your pocket! Do you deny it? You will not coerce or browbeat me, Mr. Parsons. I am a respected member of the Irish parliament and if you dare to persecute my person I will make an official complaint to the Prime Sergeant about your gross behaviour!"

"You are not above the law, Sir Buckley – nobody is," I replied.

"I AM THE LAW!" he exploded, as he overturned the table in front of me, and poked his cane in fury at my chest, eyeballing me with consummate hatred. I reeled back a step or two, caught off guard by his rapier-like movements. Saunders bounded over the counter and shouted a warning.

There was a deadly stand-off for several seconds, in which not a sound could be heard and not a muscle moved. His white eye shivered with excitement, its blood-red socket illuminating its lurid intensity. I felt sure in a personal contest he would be a formidable opponent and a match for any man. A heavy silence lingered between us, and ever so gently I tried to clear my throat.

"You don't REALLY mean that – do you, Sir Buckley?" I questioned.

The cobalt eye flashed brightly at me, and the lines in his handsome face froze hard. He did not blink at all, and he stood motionless for what seemed an interminable age. The whole time he kept that baleful orb fixed upon me, and then slowly, like someone coming out of a trance, he lowered his cane to his side. His rage had subsided into compromised pride, and without a word he turned sharply on his heels, and cut across the floor and out the tavern doors, his retinue of followers close behind him. I gasped to think that all this while I had nothing more than an extended finger in my pocket for protection, and congratulated myself on my fortitude. I had also won a crucial move in this deadly game of nerves, and with some satisfaction I muttered to myself –

"Got you!"

I proceeded to pick up the table on which Buckley had vented his spleen, while Saunders tidied up the bar area where the Kearney brothers had made their presence felt. Just as I restored my tankard to its rightful place, the leather apron of Harry Maguire stood in front of me, with the broad shoulders of Sean Matthews by his side. I prepared myself for a possible deluge of abuse from both of them. There was a long tentative pause, before the innkeeper pulled on his nose, while coughing self-consciously.

"Mr. Parsons!" he said to me, his cheeks flushing, "on behalf of my daughter and myself, can I express a sincere thanks and debt of gratitude for what you did yesterday to save Cathy and Sean from certain peril. Neither of them would be alive but for your courage, foresight, and selflessness. I misjudged you the other day and for that I apologise, Sir. You have shown yourself to be a man of honour and great decency. Once again just this minute you spared us certain humiliation, or much worse. Naturally we do not wish to be involved or tied into these dark affairs which have beset Glenboyne, but we will honour your goodwill, and if there is anything practical we can do to help you – you need only ask."

"Thank you, Mr. Maguire – that is most gracious of you," I replied, "and believe me when I tell you I do not wish to be a burden to you or your establishment. Please allow me to recompense you fully for any damage done to your furniture today or the night my room was attacked. I insist you take these two guineas as payment."

Before he could answer I had the coinage pressed firmly into the centre of his hand.

"But that is far too much, Sir!" he protested, "there was hardly any damage done. Sean! Step forward – what are you lurking there for? You have something to say to Mr. Parsons, have you not?"

The blue-eyed youth stared awkwardly at me, tossing back his pigtail with an air of challenged pride. His expression was a confused mixture of disdain and attempted cordiality. He looked most uncomfortable as he took a step towards me.

"Thank you!" he blurted shamefacedly.

I smiled and nodded at him in acknowledgement, while he returned my gesture with a brisk dip of his head. He then retreated to the bar where a beaming Cathy Maguire hugged him tenderly, clearly delighted at the outcome.

XII

A WINDOW ON THE PAST

"You wanted some information?"

"That is correct."

"Of a most particular nature, you said?"

"Of a Jack Buckley nature."

"What do you want to know?"

"Everything and anything you can tell me about the man. Who is he? What does he do? Where does he go? Who does he meet? Why is he feared?"

It was early that afternoon, and I had asked Harry Maguire to join with me and Fr. Moynihan for a private conference in the monk's bedroom. After his declaration of co-operation in the bar, I felt it was time to risk pressing him on what he might or may not know. He was decidedly reluctant to agree, but now he stood before us with his squat fingers twitching nervously and his ruddy features perspiring greatly. The three of us were completely alone.

"You realise that if he gets the slightest knowledge

that I have uttered a single syllable to you, I am as good as a dead man, Mr. Parsons – little more than a carcass to be hung out for the sport of his own crows? It is to risk not only my own neck but possibly the lives of my dear loved ones. He will stop at nothing to obliterate any words spoken against him, and would burn us out of house and home until every speck of ash had been scattered to the wind."

"I admire your bravery, Mr. Maguire, and I give you my solemn oath that not a thing you say will pass my lips or Fr. Moynihan's – who is bound to the same secrecy that I am. It is my sole desire to protect you and all the good citizens of this neighbourhood, and any information that you can supply may help to save other lives. Besides, has the time not come to stand up against this growing shadow? Proceed at your own pace and tell me what you can. If you feel unsafe or compromised – I will not press you on the matter."

Whilst listening to my entreaty his agitated eyes had been rolling in their sockets, darting quickly from my gaze, to the monk's, and back again. I could not gauge who he trusted less – me an English official, or the cloth of his own kinsman? But finally after much reflection, he appeared to settle down, and his lips quivered with determined resolution.

"Jack Buckley is a base, contemptible scoundrel, and is feared and hated by all throughout this parish. He is a wealthy aristocrat from an old protestant family, and there has always been a Buckley at Montpelier Hall, the seat of his ancestors, for as long as anyone can remember. He is the owner of every river, rock, farm, and house, from Caldbeck's Castle on the borders of Wicklow, to the marshes of Glendoo Wood, and as far as the slopes of Killakee Mountain, near the edge of Glenboyne. How the Buckleys came to own such a large estate is not clear, but it is still contended by the older folks hereabouts that his grandfather, Sir Neville Buckley, had become fabulously wealthy from the forfeited Jacobite properties taken from the Catholic landowners in the last great war.

"Much blood was spilled in those terrible years of struggle, and to this day the name of Buckley is cursed and reviled by every farmer and tenant who tills his land. They blame his forebears for their current poverty and the seizure of their rightful homesteads.

"The village is his, too, and we must all pay him rent on our properties. He is a ruthless landlord and has shown no mercy in the ravages of these last two winters. Hunger and disease have gone unchecked throughout the countryside, with the crops failing each season. The fields have become a barren wasteland where neither seed nor root will grow, and the only potatoes turned in the soil are rotten with blight. The grain storehouses are running low because the harvests could not be collected, and this October the frosts have come early making it difficult to till the land for next spring. Even the wolf has returned to the upper valleys, driven to prey on hapless livestock, where once it never dared to forage. But desperation has brought their packs closer to the village, where a constant watch is now kept to fend off any attacks. What paltry provisions are left to us in Glenboyne will surely not see us through to the new year. And what does that reprobate do? Does he show his own people some compassion? Not a hope.

"He has continued to increase our rents, and has thrown those out of doors that have fallen into arrears. The unfortunates that have refused to leave their premises – he has set his agents upon them, forcing whole families to be evicted, kicking in their doors, smashing what little furnishings they own, and putting them out onto the hardships of the road. All of this, while Buckley himself continues to live in ease and affluence, with nothing but scant regard for the suffering and oppression of his tenant farmers. Curse his hide! But most scurrilous of all are those two ruffians of his – the Kearney brothers."

"Yes, I have already had the dubious pleasure of their acquaintance," I admitted.

"Indeed – wherever Buckley goes you will find them in his wake. They are his two payed henchmen and the organisers of all that is rotten or corrupt throughout this district. He employs them to collect his monies, and if necessary to terrorise and intimidate all those who dare oppose him. It is widely suspected that they are responsible for the recent outburst of burnt cottages in the neighbouring glens, where mysterious fires have been started, under cover of night by unseen hands. Oh – but you won't catch them in the act – oh no – they are too cunning by far. They never stray for long periods from the walls of Montpelier Hall, where their master has provided them with a small adjoining plot on the side of the mountain. Both brothers are in charge of many hired farmhands armed to the hilt, and ready to do Buckley's bidding. The Kearneys often frequent my establishment before doing the rounds of their rent collections, and there is little I can do to repel them from entering. I must suffer the indignity of their visits. You may remember they were even in my tavern at the moment Sean burst into the bar when he told us Nan Harold's body had been found? I had not long filled their tankards when Sean arrived. They were seated in the lean-to at the rear of the parlour."

"Yes, I do remember two persons slipping quietly out of the bar shortly after Sean's commotion; but I could not make out their faces at the time," I recalled. "So it was they?"

"For certain," continued the innkeeper, "and it is likely they immediately informed their master of your presence at the inn. But of the things I have told you so far about Buckley, these are nothing compared to what I now must tell you. The collection of excessive rents, and the abuse of his own people are the least of his vices."

"You are referring to his suspected involvement in The Hellfire Club?" I suggested.

"What can you tell me about its history? Speak freely. I know it is difficult."

At the mention of the name the landlord's face grew white with fear, and his whole figure began to shake fretfully. The mutton-like complexion seemed to freeze into a waxen effigy, while his hands made the sign of the cross repeatedly above his forehead.

"In order to do that, Mr. Parsons, I will have to open a window on the past, if you have the patience to listen? Up to now everything I have related to you concerning this man, is only about his current activities. But the person he became was moulded a long time ago."

"Of course," I said, "please continue. The past is most pertinent."

"Rumours that such a club existed began almost seventeen years ago, when Jack's father, Sir Richard Buckley, was still alive and keeper of Montpelier Hall. He was a robust and vigorous man with a passion for hunting and keeping horses. But when his wife died of a tragic riding accident, Sir Richard drowned his sorrows in the company of gin and card games. Jack was only a teenager at the time – barely a young man.

"No one believed Sir Richard would remain long in such a dejected condition, but the alcohol slowly took control of his mind, and weakened his better judgement. Before the sod had even settled on her grave, Sir Richard had become a reckless drunkard, and it was his wont to invite the most dissolute members of the local gentry to join him in excessive bouts of drinking. These midnight meetings held no significance at first, but they assumed a more sinister aspect when the bonfires began."

"Tell me more about these bonfires," I asked.

"Well, Mr. Parsons, my own father – God rest his soul – was still alive then, when, on one Halloween night, as we left our premises, we saw great flames leaping high above Montpelier Hill, and a din of noise could be heard coming from the mountaintop. There was nothing strange in this, as it was Halloween after all, but it was when the bonfires continued after October of that year, that suspicions began to spread throughout the district.

"During these months cattle began to disappear, at first one by one, and then in larger numbers, with angry farmers pointing the finger of blame at Sir Richard. Countless sheep were also found in the vales with their throats torn out, and stable lads claimed they saw Sir Richard's labourers making off up the hillside with several of their stock. Of course their protestations could never go very far, because the farmers knew that if they pressed Sir Richard too hard – he would throw them off the land and make them quite destitute.

"The killings went on for many months, until one night two brave farmers near Glendoo Wood decided to climb Montpelier Hill for themselves, to investigate these bonfires. The following day they told several of the villagers in Glenboyne what they had seen. Under cover of the darkness, and hidden amongst the woods that border Montpelier's great Hall, they say they witnessed a disgusting spectacle. Through the trees a circle of naked people could be seen, carrying torches around the blazing pyre. With their bodies smeared in blood, the frenzied revellers seemed to be involved in some sick Satanic ritual, involving several butchered cattle that had been impaled above the burning timbers. The stench and putrefaction of the scene shocked the hidden onlookers, and they fled in terror back down the hillside, to the safety of their farms."

"How extraordinary!" I observed. "I had something of a similar nightmare myself just this morning as I slumbered in your tavern. But I must put it down to an over-active imagination, your excellent mead, and my own exhaustion. Both I and Fr. Moynihan witnessed ample first-hand evidence of bonfires at Montpelier yesterday, and I am sure this contributed to my strange dream. Under stress our thoughts and fears can play havoc with the mind, wouldn't you agree, Mr. Maguire? The power of suggestion can be a lethal influence. Not that I deny the potency or vividness of my vision – but I always try to look for a more rational explanation. For example, do you yourself believe what these fellows say they witnessed seventeen years ago? Is it not possible that they invented such fantastic tales to whip up further hatred against Sir Richard and the Buckleys, who by your own admission are a despised family in this area?"

"There is some sense in what you suggest, Mr. Parsons, and I did not myself meet the men in question; but my father did, and he swore to me that their account rang true, and each one of them was known throughout this community as a hard working individual of impeccable honesty and integrity. In any case, the events that developed in the months after this experience, only added weight to their assertions – as the killing and disappearance of livestock continued. Fear and unease soon gripped Glenboyne, as talk of devil worship spread further afield. During this time it was said that Sir Richard corrupted and debased the young Jack by involving him in the ways of the club, and brutalizing him all the while. One month Jack was universally blamed for the disappearance of two vagrants from Glenboyne, and was accused rightly or wrongly of their murders. They had been passing through the village looking for work, and had slept in the open for several nights in the ruins of Maul's Tower.

"Jack had been seen quarrelling with the two men on the morning they had planned to leave, kicking one of them to the ground, with several of his bullies to aid him. Whatever passed between him and these travellers, nobody knows – but they were never seen or heard of again. They simply vanished. Some of their clothes were found a few days later, down near the river covered in blood stains, but no one could prove that Jack had done away with them. Loose tongues even suggested that he had taken them to Montpelier Hill to be used in some form of human sacrifice, and rumours persisted that this was in fact what had happened.

"The tension throughout the neighbourhood increased, and not long after Sir Richard himself committed one of his worst atrocities. On the grounds of Montpelier Hill, close to the great Hall and its environs, there was an ancient stone circle and sacred burial ground, said to have been built by the druids in ages past. In a drunken stupor, during one of his midnight orgies, Sir Richard was goaded on by members of the club, who dared him to pull it down and have the space cleared for a new stable. The site had been much beloved for many centuries by the native community, who often prayed there on certain festivals. Imagine their outrage when Sir Richard ordered his workmen to pull the stones down, and have them removed to a quarry to be broken up? He completed the desecration by flattening the mound of earth and erecting a new shelter for his horses. This intensified the hatred of the common people against him. Some days later a fierce storm flattened his structure and took the roof clean off. The event was seen by many in the neighbourhood as divine retribution for having interfered with a spiritual landmark. Whatever blew it down, Sir Richard was not inclined to build on it again, and he left the spot abandoned for the rest of his days. Not that this was his only maltreatment of religious sites or spiritual persons. That is...well...you know...you know what... what it is I speak of, Father..."

Here the innkeeper's voice trailed off nervously as he cast an anxious look towards Fr. Moynihan. I turned to the black monk, hopeful for an explanation.

"Yes, I know what it is you wish to convey, Harry. What Mr. Maguire is trying to tell you, Daniel, is that when I was ordained as a young priest, I was sent by my order to serve on loan for several months in the parish of Glenboyne. I met Sir Richard only once, when I objected to his public flogging of a young farmhand who had stolen some bread from a storehouse. My superior of the time, Fr. Murray, advised me not to interfere in the matter, but in the passion of my convictions I attempted to stop the punishment on the appointed day in the village square. Sir Richard showed no respect for my cloth, and spurned my entreaties with a lash of his riding crop. And only for the intervention of his manservants on my behalf – he probably would have whipped me to within an inch of my life. Soon after I was moved to a parish in Dublin, and to this day I still bear the scar of that blow on my neck."

"Now I know why Buckley described you as no ordinary monk when he jeered at you in the market-place," I noted.

"And your act of courage and kindness is still remembered, Father, by those in Glenboyne whose memory recalls that day. My parents always spoke highly of your personal integrity," added the rotund proprietor.

"Thank you, Harry," replied the cleric blushing. "But return now to your account of events. You have the advantage over Mr. Parsons and me, because I left Glenboyne before those vagrants you spoke of disappeared, and certainly before Sir Richard tore down the circle of stones. That must be at least sixteen years ago by my reckoning – you can be sure of it! But for how long did these malicious activities continue that you have described to us?"

"After you departed the village, Father, all that I have outlined happened over the course of a year. Then, just as suddenly as they began, the bonfires, the midnight gatherings, and the assaults – they all ended. This would be close on fifteen years ago. Gossip had it that Sir Richard had been taken seriously ill, and during his recovery had repented of his ways, and disbanded the club.

"Whatever was the cause, the sinful rake was a changed man, and he became a reclusive figure, rarely leaving the confines of Montpelier's walls on the mountaintop. He even appeared to have turned to God, because for many years after his conversion, he was seen on occasion to attend the Reverend Hearne's chapel, sometimes in secrecy, and never speaking to a soul. Jack was sent to the continent during these years to complete his education, and it is believed he travelled far and wide, living the life of a profligate gentleman. Whether he had been banished by his father to wander abroad, or he had gone of his own free will – nobody knows.

"Peace returned to Glenboyne, and Sir Richard left his tenants and farmers unmolested. Indeed as the memories of the club receded, confidence returned gradually to the community, and crops and tillage began to thrive. You can imagine the relief we all felt that the dark days were over – or so we hoped. It continued like this for well over a decade, until without warning Jack returned from his exile two years ago. There was consternation in the community on hearing of his arrival, and great uncertainty as to his intentions. He looked as fiendish as ever, with a heart as black as pitch, and it was no coincidence that he had come back at the start of two years of crop failure and pending famine. Clearly Sir Richard must have summoned him back to manage the estate in these hard times. But if he had hoped to check his son's cruel excesses, he was sorely mistaken.

"Because this was the beginning of the excessive rents and brutal evictions that I have described to you already. Over the last two years Sir Richard was never seen and it was assumed that either he was too sick to leave Montpelier Hill, or worse, that his son kept him there against his will. And then, three months ago, our worst fears were realised. It was put out that Sir Richard had died suddenly, and his estate and lands were passed to his cursed son, who also inherited his father's hereditary title, and is now Sir Jack Buckley of Montpelier Hall. Jack's appearances in the village have increased substantially since then, and he is often seen down at Tom Farrell's forge (he is our local blacksmith), having inherited his father's passion for hunting and horsemanship. If he can't go there himself he sends Lundy in his place. He certainly cares more for his nags and stallions than for any human being. Now if only you could be a fly on that smithy's walls, I bet you could learn more about Buckley's activities than I could ever tell you. But old Tom is dour and saturnine and you will be lucky if you get a word out of him. For several weeks after Sir Richard's funeral nothing much happened. But then...Oh dear sweet God..."

The landlord's frame quivered in anguish as his hands gripped the sides of his head, tugging at his hair in a fit of upheaval. With a supreme effort he restored himself to calm and resumed his deliberations.

"It was then that these vile murders began and the bonfires were seen once again to light up the midnight skyline. Those poor sweet girls! What could they possibly have done to deserve such a terrible end, Mr. Parsons? In recent weeks strange noblemen in unmarked carriages have passed through the village in their ascent to Buckley's domain. Who they are and what business they have there can only be surmised. But I would put my life on it that Jack has reformed The Hellfire Club to deadly purpose and with an evil intent. It was after the first slaughter of Mary O' Dwyer that whispers circulated of a dreadful creature – a huge beast of some kind, that has been glimpsed or heard close to where the bodies were found. It has petrified the entire parish."

Here the publican leaned towards me and clasped his hands together in a gesture of supplication.

"You must help us, Mr.Parsons! You must! Buckley will be the death of us all. He and his father's black arts have cursed this land, and God I fear has sent his vengeance to strike us down, one by one, to punish us for their blasphemies. A malignant power has been unleashed upon us, this thing that lurks amongst the trees. Find what it is and kill it. But what if...? If it cannot be destroyed? Supposing...?"

He paused momentarily.

"Supposing it is the Evil One himself?"

I stood up and placed a comforting hand on the trembling man's shoulder.

"Calm yourself, Mr. Maguire. Your prayers I'm sure will be answered, and you must not distress yourself by dwelling on these matters, especially when so much is still unclear. What you have described has been most helpful, and know this – that whatever it is out there – if it answers to a bullet or the hangman's noose – we will have it."

Before the publican could continue any further, a distinctive tread of feet approached the bedroom from the passage outside, followed by a gentle rapping at the door.

"Father! It is I – Cathy. There are some customers looking for you."

"And now gentlemen, I have lingered too long, and doubtless said too much. If you will excuse me, I must return to my business. Please guard well what I have told you."

With this comment he departed us, and I closed the door after him. I sat down beside the cowled Benedictine, who rubbed his chin vigorously in deep rumination.

"What do you make of it all, Father? It is a sordid business, is it not? And it certainly ties in with what you discovered at Montpelier – not to mention the jaw bones you saw in the furnace! That would explain why the bonfires are so extensive, if he is burning cattle for some sick ceremony."

"I agree, Daniel, and it gives further meaning to the use and discovery of the runes. I have no doubt in my mind that everything we have learnt in the last few days is connected by a common thread. However, we still have no binding evidence of Buckley's involvement in these deaths – it remains unproven speculation. But I do believe the truth is up on Montpelier Hill, safe and hidden somewhere, and you will have to find a way to get up there again, this time secretly, without Buckley's knowledge, to catch him in whatever sordid business he is fermenting. Perhaps a midnight expedition under cover of darkness could reveal everything?"

"I like your strategy, Father, but we would need a guide, someone who knows the terrain intimately, who could get us up and back unnoticed. Not an easy task with these wolf packs on the prowl, and I suspect that it was the Kearney brothers who tried to torch my room the other night. They may strike again. Why else would they have made such pointed comments to me on the mountaintop? Subtlety is not one of their strengths."

"Very likely it was them," agreed the priest, "and you can be sure they are watching our every move boy!"

"If there was some way of getting one of Buckley's own servants on our side," I continued, "one of them at least must surely know everything that is going on up there. No doubt he has dissenters in his own camp, who only follow him through fear."

"A good point," nodded the monk. "So let us pray that God may reveal such a person to us soon. Meantime we must keep a watchful eye on his attendants and probe their weaknesses."

XIII

A REMARKABLE LEATHER BELLOWS

The innkeeper's description of Tom Farrell had aroused my curiosity and convinced me that a trip to his workshop could be informative. Within the hour we made our way on horseback to Maul's Tower to visit the blacksmith's forge, which was attached to the western edifice of the Norman ruins. Using the beasts that Wilkinson had acquired for us, I rode with Fr. Moynihan, while Saunders followed us broadside with several mounted redcoats in his train. I had not been in the saddle since leaving Knutsford in Cheshire, and my legs took a little bit of adjusting to the familiar chaffing of the horse's motion. But at last we had some mobility, and how marvellous it was to feel a sturdy mare under ones legs after so many days of having to walk through dangerous territory. To my delight the black monk was a complete natural in the stirrup, commanding his colt authoritatively as though he had just broken him to the rein.

A din of jackdaws circled the ivied battlements and the crash of metal could be heard below them, where smoke and steam rose steadily from the thatched roof of the smithy's work space. By a stroke of luck our approach had not been noticed. Sensing an opportunity I ordered everyone to dismount, and we left the track in order to cut across a patch of briars in front of the northern aspect of the tower. Here we could hide the horses undetected, watched over by one of the soldiers, while the rest of us crept stealthily through the shell of the fortress to the western side. The great buttressed walls had crumbled in places where cannon or decay had wrought their ruin, and through one such hole it was possible to hide unseen with an almost perfect view of the blacksmith's activities and just within earshot. I signalled to Saunders for quiet, and peering through this aperture both I and Fr. Moynihan craned our necks to listen and observe.

Clearly this smithy dated from the original Norman settlement and had somehow survived the passing of the centuries. Several thatched sheds and barns encompassed a rough courtyard of dirty straw, with the original medieval granite walls still intact around the enclosure. Despite the chill of an October afternoon an enormous furnace blazed fiercely at the back of the yard where a young lad operated a remarkable leather bellows, while an old man – presumably the blacksmith – hammered zealously on a massive anvil, turning a piece of raging white metal. But a movement from the front of the workshop made my heart leap, as I detected Jack Buckley, his men, and the Kearney brothers, all standing close to their coach, waiting impatiently, while Lundy made with haste towards the master of the forge. The fates were shining on us, as here at last was a chance to play cat to Buckley's mouse and hope that he would reveal something.

"Is it ready yet, Tom?" growled the dwarf. "Sir Jack is in bad form terday."

The august figure of Tom Farrell turned slowly, revealing an old weathered face, tanned from years of outdoor labour, with white sideburns down to his chin, puffing on a dirty pipe, which clung to one corner of a sunken aged mouth. Despite his stooped gait there remained a considerable vigour and energy to his arms and shoulders. An enormous leather apron covered his body from chest to knee, with similar padding tied to his shins for protection. A nest of yellow-white hair sat untidily above his pinched glowering eyes.

"By Chreest – it's a comin! It's a comin! Sure when is he ever in good form, blast him?" he wheezed in response.

"Never mind dat - did ye repair it for im?"

"Course I did! And near broke me back too doing it!"

"C'mon den! C'mon! Give it to me!" urged the tiny coachman, "and make sure dose udder horseshoes are ready be termorrow."

Something large, heavy, long and bulky, wrapped in filthy sackcloth, was handed by the apprentice boy into Lundy's hands. In his eagerness to take it the package slipped out of the midget's greasy fingers and fell with a clank onto the hay-strewn ground. Cursing at this clumsiness Buckley raced across the courtyard.

"YOU STUPID LITTLE BASTARD!" he bellowed in explosive rage.

Then brandishing a riding crop he lashed out with venomous bile at his diminutive servant, assaulting him with several blows across his back and shoulders.

"Can't you do anything right you worthless runt? Pick it up! PICK IT UP I SAID! If it is damaged I will smash every bone in your sorry body."

This invective was accompanied by a vicious kick from Buckley's boot, which caused Lundy to drop to his knees. But with a rapid reflex reaction the dwarf sprang back up, ripping from his jacket a small hidden knife, his teeth clenched together, and his eyes ablaze with fabulous hatred. Thrusting the blade at his master's legs he failed to land a fatal blow, only grazing Sir Jack's silk breeches. Then a struggle between the two ensued for some seconds, like two wild badgers fighting in a pit. The black felt hat flew off Buckley's head, and with athletic precision he kicked the weapon out of Lundy's grasp, sending it flying across the enclosure. Seizing his attacker by the throat he lifted the squat figure with a single arm and pinned him up against the wall, his cobalt eye seething with malignancy.

"Filthy rat – you couldn't even knife me right! Vile scrag-end! Did you think you might outwit me – a champion of the blade? Hah! – you couldn't stab your own master even if I held the blade for you! I ought to tar you right now and set your flesh alight – or strip you naked and throw you into a pit of thorns. But not yet – no, that would be too easy. I have other uses for you, and will devise your special punishment at a more appropriate moment soon. Just remember I own you and the dirty hovel that I let you live in. Nor ever forget that everything you have is mine, and I can make your family suffer too. MICK!"

"Yes, Sir Jack!"

"Pick up that package and get it into the coach. You will take the reins as driver back to Montpelier and keep a close eye on this traitorous dog."

Here he flung Lundy to the ground like discarded offal. Although humiliated I could see the passion of revenge still shining brightly in the dwarf's eyes. There was a peculiar calm to his hatred which I did not understand. Whilst I was shocked at what I had observed, I was not sure of my jurisdiction in this matter, as Lundy was after all in the employment of his master. We were also still outnumbered by Buckley's crew, so I thought it best to wait and observe, and not intervene.

"And as for you!" said Buckley with cutting scorn, turning his heinous eye on Tom Farrell, "don't I pay you enough for your services? Make sure those horse-shoes are shod by this time tomorrow, and none of your slacking – do you hear?"

A sardonic grunt came from the blacksmith, in acknowledgement of the order, his thick-set eyebrows bristling with indignation. Impatient to get away, the tall aristocrat clapped his hands and re-ascended the steps of the vehicle, signalling to the footmen to depart. In a trice they were gone, the black coach and riders making furiously towards Glenboyne. We waited some minutes until they were well out of sight, and then circumnavigating the western walls of the battlements in silence, we dropped by suddenly to the smithy's yard, with Tom Farrell looking as if he had been taken by a seizure. His shock and displeasure at our appearance could not be disguised, as he stared blankly at us like a stuffed scarecrow.

I used the excuse that we needed one horse to be shod quickly to explain away our visit, which he set to doing immediately, while Fr. Moynihan cast his eagle eye around the premises. I thanked him for the horses that Wilkinson had borrowed, although he frowned copiously at the mention of this. Based on Harry Maguire's account of him I knew it would be pointless to interrogate the blacksmith, so I plied him instead with necessary pleasantries and a dozen platitudes on the nobility of the farrier's trade. But he was no fool, and eyed me suspiciously all the while, replying only in snorts. He had the horseshoe done in no time, and through the corner of my eye I sensed that the black monk was ready to depart. Without delay we set off down the track where we re-joined Saunders and his mounted men. The Benedictine's hazel-brown eyes twinkled brightly with a suffused air of confident conviction.

"Did you spot something?" I enquired.

"Well – did you notice that bellows was of rather large proportions? Quite enormous it seemed. Why would he need something that powerful just to make horseshoes? There were iron bands too welded into the strangest of shapes, and one was as long as a spear! And that package? There was something important in it – very important. All odd work for a blacksmith. Don't you see – there is some relationship between him and the master of Montpelier?"

"I think you have something there, Father, and we must needs keep an eye on this Tom Farrell without arousing his suspicion. Let's follow Buckley and his mob back to the village – perhaps we can watch them from a distance."

We set off at a steady gallop and followed the path that clung to the river's edge. The row of listless cabins that had guided us to visit Dr. Hannon's cottage could be seen close by, and using them as a pointer we found our way back onto the stony track that ascended to the marketplace. Passing the grain house we descended onto the main thoroughfare of the village, where several carts and wagons trundled along the great wooden planks, completing their business for the day. A mist of tiny raindrops was now evident, which helped to bring on the growing shadows of dusk's gathering gloom. How pleased I was to see the regal contours of Harkin's splendid coach pulled up outside a small dilapidated shop, with Wilkinson and his men standing in a circle of guard close by. But as we approached them my joy did not last long, as I noticed that their attention was not on me, but on a gathering of townsfolk just beyond the vehicle, where I could hear turmoil and a good deal of shouting. Several redcoats were trying to restore order; I could distinguish the raised voices of at least thirty villagers, their faces grim with fear and loathing. Dismounting from our horses, Fr. Moynihan and I approached the strange spectacle.

"Wilkinson! Good to see you are returned safely. Any further news from Colonel Butler about those reinforcements? Did your search at Kelly's Gorge bear any fruit? And what is all this fracas about? What is going on here, man?"

The Corporal stepped up to present himself, and in a lowered voice said;

"Im pleased to tell you, Mr. Parsons, that the company of men which you requested may be here tomorrow. We met a scout from the detachment not one hour back, and he confirmed that the road was almost fully cleared and that the soldiers were camping close by. They should be in Glenboyne hopefully tomorrow afternoon – or very soon after."

"Thank God for that!" I exclaimed in relief.

"We also managed to find Private Taylor's jacket this time," continued Corporal Wilkinson, "which I have kept in the back of Harkin's coach, but we found no sign of his person or body."

"But it still gives us hope that he may yet be alive! He could be captive somewhere – held prisoner against his will – or even injured and unable to move."

"True, Sir! It is a possibility, I agree. With regard to this business *here*, Sir, it is not good at all. We only arrived back in the village ourselves moments ago. It happened before we got here, Sir!"

"What do you mean? What happened?" I said nervously.

Before he could answer me, the unruly throng had pushed past the infantry, and sensing their anger I stepped forward to engage with them. My heart sank as the distraught features of Sean Matthews burst through the crowd, his face contorted with anguish, and his eyes red with tears. He shook tremulously as though all his strength was sapped from him, and tried to command his voice before addressing me.

"My beloved Cathy is gone! Sweet Jesus! They have taken my only life and love! They have stolen the very heart of me. Not my lovely Cathy – oh please, don't let them take her away..."

My heart began to pound as I heard his words, and an overwhelming sense of dread and anger rose inside me.

"What are you talking about, Sean? Look at me, for heaven's sake! Who has taken her? When?"

"The fiend of Montpelier Hall grabbed her!" he quivered, "that monster Buckley and his vile circle of scum. Who else do you think? She had only left Nan's funeral and was returning from the Reverend Hearne's chapel – I thought she had already made it back to the tavern – when his fancy black coach pulled up alongside, and dragged her in through the door kicking and screaming!"

"Now be careful, Sean," interrupted Fr. Moynihan, "were you there yourself? Did you see it with your own eyes? You must be absolutely certain."

"Yes, Father," he affirmed, "I had just visited the hop store when I heard a commotion outside the rectory at the base of the road. I could see young Eoin McKeogh pointing in alarm at the four plumed horses and recognised Buckley's transport and his train of men. It happened so quickly I could barely react – but I saw Cathy call out for aid, and ran as fast as my feet would carry me. But it was too late. They had hoisted her into the vehicle and had already passed out through the turnpike gate. Poor Eoin was so upset – he saw it all too. Didn't you, Eoin?"

Amongst the gathered bystanders a scruffy young farm boy was sobbing uncontrollably next to his father, his face blackened with the soil of many tears.

"Is that true, my brave fello?" I queried.

He nodded his matted hair furiously at me, and broke into a fresh bout of convulsions.

"Tis true... tis true..." he gave back, stammering awkwardly, "de bad man took her...de bad man from de mountain! He gave her some kind uv a biscuit. But she did not like it – she threw it away on de ground!"

I felt a nausea take a grip of me, and Fr. Moynihan's face turned an ashen grey. As if sensing our thoughts Sean turned his powerful frame towards us, and pulled out a rag from his pocket. Thrusting the cloth towards my face, he used it to hold aloft a small object.

"You know what he gave her, Mr. Parsons!" he expounded. "This was discovered on the ground where she had dropped it – the devil's witchcraft! The mark of DEATH!"

With his hand trembling, he held the tiny rune up to my eyes. It had the same sinister symbol etched deeply in its oval centre, and was identical to that which the Benedictine had shown me in the field. The marking was a clear black stroke delineated thus:

ᛉ

The result of his action was immediate panic, as the gang of onlookers gasped in naked terror, bolting in every direction as though fleeing for their lives. The

English prude in me felt somehow riled by what I perceived as their cowardice, and a certain irritability got the better of me.

"Come back!" I pleaded, "why do you take flight? There is nothing to fear. It is a mere foolish trinket given by a cheap peddler of tricks to frighten the vulnerable. You must trust to common sense and not give in to madness!"

"He is right!" shouted Fr.Moynihan. "Listen to me – running away will not resolve anything. You must all stand together and show strength, or your imaginations will take control. Your faith is clear – witchcraft and sorcery can have no power over you, so do not give in to pagan threats."

But the Corkman's words went unheeded by the petrified listeners, who dissolved quickly into the growing darkness.

"She will DIE, Father! – be torn asunder just like the others," yelled Sean, "we must rescue her now! Let us storm Montpelier Hill tonight, Mr. Parsons, and stop this foul beast. This is his revenge for not receiving his rent. For the love of God, we must do something fast!"

"I am as horrified and disgusted as you, Sean – believe me," I replied, "and I will do everything in my power to save her. But understand that Buckley outnumbers us considerably, and if we attempt an attack on his stronghold tonight – he will not only be ready, but he will pick us off one by one until he has massacred every last soul. Under darkness too – it would be the perfect trap from which he could ambush us and defend his position. Tomorrow a relief company of men will be here, and as soon as they arrive I will commence a full and immediate assault on Montpelier's walls to find her. You have my word, Sean – and have I not shown you that I can be trusted?"

The splendid youth wrung his hands in his hair, and tried to control the burgeoning emotions that consumed his heart. To give him full credit he mastered his pain, and with dignity he said softly –

"Indeed – you have been decent to us, Sir, and I will not deny it. Nor will I forget the great turn you did for me and Cathy last evening. To think now that it is all undone."

"You must not speak like that!" I retorted. "Nothing is undone – nothing is so final. Come back with me now to the tavern and we will make a plan of action for tomorrow's business. In the meantime I appeal to you not to discuss these runes further, nor to give any belief to them. Promise me not to mention their name in public, as to do so will create fear, and that begets panic."

He assented to my plea, and the black monk put a

comforting arm around his shoulder and proceeded with him back to the inn. The street was now all but silent and a glorious moon burst forth where the heavy clouds had parted, its silver disk basking brightly in a patchwork of delicate rain pools. Harkin drove the coach into the courtyard of the tavern, and we agreed that both the conveyance and the horses should use this as their base, until our business in the village was concluded.

A scene of potent grief greeted us in the lounge area, where a harrowed Harry Maguire rocked to and fro in tremulous heartache for his missing daughter. No words of assurance from me could make any impression upon his mind, but both Sean and the robed cleric succeeded somewhat in calming him. The sight of this man crying like a child, and the plight that he now faced, struck a deep chord inside me. I felt ashamed and guilty that this had happened under my watch, and I regretted not having been present to prevent it. But I knew that to berate myself would only darken my thoughts and drain my energy for the terrible task that lay ahead of us on the morrow.

Retreating to a small storage room at the back of the building, I held counsel with Wilkinson, Saunders, and Fr. Moynihan. We discussed all tactical options and I instructed those present that if anything should happen to either me, or indeed any of them, the attack was still to go ahead. If I was injured Wilkinson would take charge of the men, and would act under Colonel Butler's command when he arrived. Buckley was to be arrested, and any resistance by his militia was to be dealt with by force. If fired upon, we would return fire. Montpelier Hall was to be searched from top to bottom until all its secrets were revealed and Cathy found. The brave monk requested that he accompany us, but I warned him that I could not guarantee his safety. If he did come, he was to stay well behind the firing line, and to obey the instructions of the soldiers. On no account was he to enter Montpelier Hall until the manoeuvres were finished and the building made safe. Satisfied with these plans, I then suggested that we retire to our rooms and get what rest we could.

I found my own chamber cold and cheerless, and occupied myself by bathing my wound with fresh salts and water. The chest abrasion had improved considerably, so that I felt confident enough to press against it – there was no resultant bleeding. The bruise on my forehead had also mellowed and was no longer so raw in appearance. I tried to turn in, but found myself restless, my thoughts racing with dire images of Cathy's torture, or worse. How was I to sleep knowing of her desperation and suffering? As I wrestled with such feelings, it dawned on me that Wilkinson had neglected to give me Private Taylor's jacket, which he said he had left at the back of the coach. Needing to relieve myself anyway, I decided to put on my coat, and retrieve the item, without disturbing or waking the others. I hoped, too, that the missing man's clothing could contain some clue, however slight, that the Corporal may have overlooked.

Slipping down the corridor and passing the casks of ale, I found my way into the silent courtyard, where the stately vehicle stood grandly, shimmering under a gauze of moonlit beams. I did as nature required, and then noticed that beyond the walled enclosure a fiery glow lit up the skyline several miles distant. To my horror I realised that the illumination came from the direction of Buckley's domain, and I was sure these were bonfires set alight atop the summit of Montpelier Hill. The sight disturbed me with bleak and dreadful thoughts, but choosing not to dwell on them I opened the coach door and lent forward into the dull interior.

A sudden crunch on the gravel made my blood freeze, and a fraction of a second later powerful hands gripped me from behind, one of them covering my mouth before I could utter a sound. Indignant rage exploded in my veins as I wrestled to free myself and face my attackers. But extra hands joined in the ambush, and in desperation I sank my teeth into the palms that held me. A forceful kick was the response, and a hard, cold object struck me.

Dropping to the ground my arms were pinned down by heavy boots which stood upon them, whilst a bag was fitted over my head. There I remained until passing out into darkness and utter confusion.

XIV

LASCIVIOUS HANDS

When a multitude of pains assaults your body it is often difficult for the brain to register these signals, either by order of occurrence, or by merit of intensity. Which will it ignore? Which will it assuage? Such a dilemma now faced me, as my aching head tried to regain consciousness through a veil of painful physical sensations that besieged my entire frame. To say I woke up was not quite true, as I seemed for some time to drift in and out of various states of wakefulness. How long this lasted I cannot say. Mere minutes? Hours? I became acutely aware of a sharp stinging pulsation that rose from the nape of my neck to the top of my skull – undoubtedly the result of whatever had hit me. All my muscles and joints felt strained, stiff and sore, while my skin tingled with hot and freezing temperatures at the same time. Perhaps I had been drugged?

My languid eyelids tried to open repeatedly but failed to do so on successive attempts, as though the weight of ages held them down. When they did manage to part, a congregation of blurred and garish figures flashed before me, silhouetted from behind by the deep umber hues of flickering flames. A hushed tone of excited voices could be heard amongst them, punctuated with interludes of restrained tittering. In a concerted effort to rouse myself I raised my head upwards and forced my dilating pupils to open. A sinister and dire situation was promptly revealed.

My two arms were stretched out above me to their maximum length and hung in irons from a beam above my head. A glance downwards showed that my legs were similarly forced apart to their utmost width, with my ankles manacled to the floor – so that in shape I resembled perfectly the letter X. I had been stripped entirely naked but for a thin slip of cloth that barely protected my modesty. The muscles of my arms, shoulders, back, chest, abdomen, buttocks, and thighs had all been covered in a perfumed oil, which had been massaged extensively onto my skin. This accounted for a coat of beaded sweat that clung to my chest and armpits as my body did its best to regulate escaping moisture. I realised all too horribly that I was a perfect prisoner and slave to my cunning captors.

As my focus slowly improved my sight penetrated the shadows of my internment, and I found myself in a chamber of impressive size with features that looked disturbingly familiar. Sitting in a semi-circle of high-backed chairs was the strangest assembly of characters that I had ever seen, each face covered by a mask, similar to those found in Venetian balls – some of grotesque designs, others beautiful. These disguises covered only as low as the nose bridge, leaving the mouths free with gaps for the eyes. From the throat down to the feet each person was draped in heavy silken robes of a scarlet red which covered their persons completely. They all sat in a similar pose with their hands face downwards and resting on their knees.

Behind them leaped the yellow glowing tongues of a roaring fireplace, its capacious grate crackling with gigantic tree logs. The massive arched alcoves of deep-set masonry on either side were of medieval proportions. At its apex a protruding mantelpiece of ancient carved stone hemmed it in, creating a vortex of sparks swirling upwards towards the flue. Everywhere candles were burning from silver candelabra, creating the appearance of a lavish spectacle. And there above the hearth, where I had last observed it, was that same triangular black shield, decorated with three bulls' heads, all white in colour. It was a coat of arms not likely to be forgotten, and standing beneath it, his arms folded, and looking like a demi-god, was my nemesis – the master of Montpelier; for it was in his banqueting parlour that I now hung in chains.

Buckley, too, wore a high collared cloak of crimson hue, which, upon my awakening, he removed and handed to a servant. A sparkling red waistcoat of fine-spun silk was revealed beneath, embossed with silver twist and black satin patterns. A white laced shirt with frilled cuffs hung from his arms, while around his neck he wore a tidy white cravat held in place by a gold neck-tie. His greying locks rested on his shoulders like a royal mane and he looked taller than on previous occasions. He sauntered towards me with breath-taking arrogance.

"I did try to warn you! But you just WOULD NOT LISTEN!" he teased with a sneer.

An explosive revulsion for this man now surged inside me, and clenching my teeth I tensed my biceps, and began to thrash wildly to free myself. My skin chaffed where the irons held me fast, and great drops of sweat ran down my arms, chest and thighs. The more I struggled the more he grinned mockingly.

"You are MAD, Buckley!" I yelled. "Where is the girl? What have you done with Cathy Maguire? For God's sake man! Let her go! Do what you want with me, but in mercy's name release her!"

"You dare to call ME mad?" he shrieked, and raising the back of his hand he struck me full across the cheek with a heavy blow. Then grasping my chin in a vice-like grip he pressed his face up to mine.

"Shall I tell you what IS mad, Mr. Parsons? When an English pig like you sticks his nose in where it is not wanted. When a prating fool from Cheshire, ever keen to do his duty for King and country, drags his worthless bones through the Dublin Mountains because he thinks he is the law! Ha! Ha! YOU the law? As if that fat fool in Hanover, our glorious King George, would give a hog's hair for your sense of duty. He would not drop his pants to pass water on a dimwit like you. What did they tell you in Dublin Castle? Did they promise you festoons and laurels on your triumphant return with ME in chains? Were you going to enter Dublin with MY head on a pike? WERE YOU?" – he roared, belting me once again across the face.

"There are natural laws and powers in Ireland – older than all the charters of England," he continued, "the law of the land and our great ancient ancestors – the Brehon laws. It is they that hold sway over these mountains and valleys, handed down to us from our noble clansmen and chieftains of yore. They have governed our people for a thousand years, and guided us through generations of disaster and incursions. But you would not know anything about them – would you, blockhead?"

"They were outlawed a century ago," I replied, unconvinced of his allegiance to anything. "It is the English common law that prevails now."

"Not on this mountain, jackass!" he declared in triumph, while the group behind him laughed in obsequious refrain. Then turning to his requisite audience he goaded them on to further scorn.

"Just look at this buffoon!" – he pointed to me – "did you ever see anything so ridiculous? Where is your honour now, my lad? In the gutter you will find, where it will stay along with everything else when we have finished with you. And you thought not only to challenge me and trespass on my land, but that the Benedictine monkey could play truant in my outhouses? You call yourself a Protestant, Mr. Parsons? Is that what you regard as devotion to our monarch as head of the Church of England? Conspiring with a papist sympathiser against one of your own?"

"We may well both be Protestants, Buckley," I gave back, "but I am not one of your own. Fr. Moynihan is a kind, decent, noble person, filled with the dignity of the human spirit. And he has shown more courage and self-sacrifice than many other men I know. I would rather spend an eternity in his company than to suffer ten seconds of your depraved society."

He grabbed me by my hair, wrenching it backwards.

"Oh, but you will suffer, Mr. Parsons, and taste the chalice of pain. I also have a master to serve, and his needs will be fulfilled by you shortly. Since you are convinced of our lewd practices – please allow us not to disappoint. You are indeed a fine specimen of masculinity, which has not escaped the notice of my guests, and they are very keen to make your physical acquaintance. Your athletic form is most propitious to our needs and wants. Where did you get such a muscular frame?"

As he spoke gasps of erotic pleasure began to emanate from the lips of those behind him. Several began to touch themselves irreverently while their breathing became laboured as though lost in some debased sensuous reverie. What sordid business was this?

He passed a hand across my torso, while running his other up my armpit and onto my bicep. Then thrusting his face against mine, he tried to kiss me and insert his tongue into my ear. I tore my head away furiously, shaking it from side to side, but there was little I could do to repulse his vile advances. So now I knew the nature of their sick designs – to use me for deviant gratification, perhaps torture me, and most certainly kill me. I was dealing with a ruthless murderer and my execution was not far off.

"DAMN YOU TO HELL, BUCKLEY!" I roared, pulling violently at the fetters that held me.

My sinews grew taut as my body fought desperately to resist, but strong as I was my flexed limbs could only tear at their bonds. These exertions produced a profuse perspiration, which soaked my body from head to toe. Each moment of this struggle caused the perverse viewers to become more and more excited. Their heavy panting grew raucous and vulgar, as their shining eyes became fixed upon my shimmering physique. Rising from their seats they disrobed in unison, their cloaks slipping silently onto the deep-piled rug. To my consternation each of the profligate figures was stark naked, a mixture of men and women – most of them young and in the prime of their life. All remained masked. There was a majority of females in the grouping, several with curvaceous contours and shapely bodies. The youthful bucks, too, were of masculine and athletic form, and for the first time I could make out behind them other people standing in the shadows – clad in black capes, their heads hooded, morose and silent.

One of the sultry minxes stepped forward, gathering her breasts into her arms where she fondled and caressed her nipples, her eyes fixed upon me. She moaned in luxurious ecstasy as though behaving under the influence of some spell. Approaching me quickly she quivered in the thrill of expectation.

"Oh Master! Master! Has the time come?" she pleaded. "Let me touch his body – it is magnificent – I want him! Please let me have him!"

Buckley's raised hand held her back for a moment, teasing her like a pup in training, all the while her tongue twisting salaciously around the corners of her lips. But he could not restrain her long, and laughing at her frenzy – he bade her to advance.

"Very well, my dear! You have waited long enough. Now feast yourself on the beauty of his flesh. He is yours to vanquish first."

A storm of sensuality was unleashed upon me as she fell to her knees and ran her hot tongue along the hair of my naval. I tried zealously to shake her off, but she giggled at my bondage and grew more bold in her seduction. I could have railed madly against this onslaught but I was now in one of those unspeakable moments in a person's life where anything I might say or do could bring forth my immediate death. To avoid this I determined to keep my mouth shut and say absolutely nothing to provoke an early murder. My teenage years had taught me the necessity to stay calm, and if ever I needed to follow that advice it was surely now. It was essential I should play along with their refined debauchery – it was a matter of survival. Any minutes or hours that I could gain, just might give Wilkinson and his company of men enough time to liberate Montpelier; even now they could be advancing towards my aid. It was possible, too, that Buckley was unaware of this detachment on its way to Glenboyne, a thought which gave me a crumb of comfort. If only I could determine what day it was? How long had I been captive and asleep?

Remaining masked, the licentious female advanced her tongue up towards my chest, while simultaneously running her hands across my torso. Potent glee burned in those lustrous eyes as her moist lips closed on the tip of my nipple, where she sucked joyously until it became hard and aroused. This action seemed to excite her to a new level. As a nubile creature she knew her business well, and although her purpose was repugnant to me, her physical beauty could not be ignored. Her pert breasts, which she pinned against me, were ample, rounded, and hard. Those full red lips were designed to thrill and her hips were of a perfect curve. Pressing her thighs against mine she heaved up and down, up and down – like a cat in heat against a pole. Exhausted though I was, she succeeded in awakening my masculinity; sensing her triumph, she plunged downward and ripped the scant covering from my groin.

A scream of delight broke from her, and her eyes started wildly from their sockets in sheer excitement at my stimulation. Similar cries of lust exploded from the assembled throng as they gaped at my naked body. They could not contain themselves any longer, and raising a din of shrieks and grunts, like a pack of hounds they raced towards me – a dozen of them at least. Meanwhile, the woman thrust her lips lower, and finding the object of her desire, she devoured it. Back and forth, to and fro, she worked her head assiduously – to and fro, back and forth, her fingers buried deep in my loins. The others took her lead and I watched in dizzy horror as I was swamped by a sea of hands, lips and limbs, all touching, caressing, licking, feeling, their nauseous breaths reeking on my skin.

The lithe muscles of the debased youths crushed me from behind, their hardened organs rubbing playfully against my buttocks, sickening me to the core of my soul. If possible they were worse than the women, their lascivious hands and hungry lips worshipping my body shamelessly, teasing and probing, sometimes in pairs. The more I resisted the greater was their collective exultation, their actions rising to a heightened fever of arousal. This explosive rapture caused a similar excitement to ignite amongst the remaining onlookers still seated, who, throwing off their clothes, began cavorting with their naked counterparts; so that a veritable orgy now reigned throughout the banqueting hall. This was fuelled by copious libations of wine, gin and brandy, brought in by servants, until everywhere dozens of bodies rolled intertwined, spread across tables, gyrating on the floor, or in any space that allowed them satisfaction. Music played, and drums beat, with incantations chanted in seductive rhythm.

The pyramid of flesh that now enclosed me was relentless; drowsy from some opiate that I was certain had been given me, I passed out several times, only to be revived by my tormentors, again, and again. The clink of goblets, the howls of prurient pleasure, and the chuckling of whoredom – all co-mingled into a carousel of libidinous depravity. One voice above them all stood out, his cold metallic laughter rising to the roof – the stern accents of Buckley. If ever a man resembled the Devil incarnate – I was now surely looking at his smiling face.

XV

THE INITIATION

I must have slept for several hours, because when I awoke I was no longer in the nefarious parlour, but found myself in total darkness – disoriented, and in silence, lying on a stone floor. The great chamber and all its miscreants had vanished, and clearly I had been moved to some dismal dungeon where damp and cold permeated my surroundings. A rank smell of stale air and fetid straw pervaded my nostrils, whilst I spread out my arms to examine my new environment. To my relief I was no longer chained from above and my arms were free to move at will. As I stood up one leg was unchained, but the other remained manacled to the wall. In circumference I could walk but two or three paces before the shackles pulled me back, making further exploration impossible.

Mercifully, I was once again clothed – if only with a rough cloak that had been thrown about my shoulders. My breeches, which were torn and muddied, I could feel about my waist. My shoes too had been restored. Of my shirt and jacket I could find nothing, and in order not to freeze to death I would have to wrap this cape closely around my upper half. The only sound was the ponderous plopping of steady drops of moisture onto the flagstones beneath me. Set into the wall and high out of reach, I could see a tiny portal or window to the night sky, held fast by two iron bars, which revealed a single shining star in the great firmament. It was my only connection to the outside world, but I thanked my Lord and Maker for the solace that it gave me. That beautiful white gem represented what I could only dream of – my liberty.

My humiliation was now complete, and I shuddered at what had happened to me. How could I have been so careless as to leave myself vulnerable in the tavern courtyard? What stupidity! Was it now my fate to die horrendously, unseen forever by my loved ones? My parents' sweet faces appeared before my eyes, and an aching in my heart overwhelmed me. The thought that I should disappear and that they would never know how or when I died – and the distress it would cause them – filled me with dread. All manner of black and wretched thoughts raced fitfully through my mind. How easy it would be now to give in to hate – that ready bedfellow of a disturbed mind. But this is what Buckley was hoping to achieve and I was determined not to acquiesce. He could rob me of my dignity, degrade and assault my flesh, even take my life – but he would never steal the freedom of my thoughts, heart and mind.

Looking up through that slit in the masonry I could detect two other things. First, was the subtle glow of a faint red light around the edges of the stonework, which flickered in a queer pattern. This I took to be a bonfire close at hand somewhere on Montpelier Hill.

The second was the hair-raising howls, growing ever closer, of a pack of savage wolves. Obviously I could not see them – but their high-pitched reverberant yelps suggested that they were close at hand. However terrifying they sounded, there was something soulful and almost plaintive in their calls, as though they were lonely out there on that stark hillside.

The shuffle of approaching boots startled me, and the flames of a burning torch cast their light through a tiny peep-hole in my cell door. I had not expected company so soon; I listened as a key was turned and several heavy bolts were drawn back. The rusted iron door resisted stubbornly and two great heaves were needed to swing it open. My poor eyes were blinded by the torchlight and for a moment I could see nothing. Preparing myself for the worst, I primed my fists to lash out. The holder of the beacon placed it in an iron bracket on the wall and approached me. It was Lundy.

"Eat!" he grunted, kicking a soiled platter with some scraps on it across the flagstones to me. Pouring a little water from a dirty flask into a wooden bowl, he placed it at my feet. There was just enough illumination to reveal his features, which maintained a perfect rigidity and saturnine expression. I would have to risk much.

"Listen to me Lundy! Your master intends not just to kill ME – there will be many other victims. I have no idea of what you know or what you don't know, and maybe you have no direct involvement in any of his activities. Perhaps he has forced you to obey him? But understand this – everyone on Montpelier Hill who is found to be involved in his crimes, will be arrested, charged, and hanged from the gallows. My murder today or tomorrow will not stop that inevitable outcome – it will only hasten it. There will be no escape from justice. Sir Buckley is out of control - but you can help stop him!"

His beady black eyes averted my gaze as he recorked the flagon of water.

"Where is Cathy Maguire? Is she to be butchered too? If you know that she is held within these walls, then look into your soul and save her. I realise you dare not risk your own life, but you can send word to Glenboyne that she is captive here. There must be a way of alerting the locals without your master's knowledge? Think of her family and the grief they will endure! It is an abomination!"

He ignored me, but maintaining his grim expression he removed the torch from the wall and prepared to depart.

"In fact Buckley will eliminate anyone close to him who has knowledge of his criminal activities. He will not suffer them to survive – and that includes you, Lundy!"

He paused for a brief moment, and raising his eyes towards me, he fixed me with a steady cold glare.

"An jeest wat do ye tink will stop me tellin' me

Mastuur what ye jeest said, Misstuur Parsons? Huh?"
he said, glowering at me. Then spitting on the floor,
he rattled the keys and made peremptorily for the
cell door. His overt threat forced me to play my one
and only trump card.

"Because your master will not just strip you naked
and throw you into a pit of thorns! He will tear you
limb from limb in revenge for your bungled attempt
to knife him. You were seen at the blacksmith's forge
Lundy! By me and other witnesses!"

My comments stopped him in his tracks, and
jerking back his shoulders he turned on his heels in
amazement. His eyes blazed with incredulity.

"Heh? Wat do ye mean by dat? Darned ye! Ye could
na have seen or heard dat...sure I wud have seen ye
dere...how in de name of...?"

For the first time his dour demeanour became
animated and his raised eyebrows betrayed alarm. In
two minds as to what to do next, he stood motionless
at the threshold as I continued to call his bluff.

"It does not matter how we saw you..." I continued.
"Everything you said and did was seen and heard at
the smithy's – your fight with Buckley, his promise
to punish you and your family, and even... even that
PACKAGE that you dropped on the ground...oh yes...
that too was witnessed. We know what was in it!"

These last words had a powerful effect, and his face

contracted into a spasm of temper and confusion. He paced over to me and thrust the torch into my face examining my eyes. It was clear he was unsure of the extent of my knowledge and I played on this crucial advantage.

"I am convinced that you are innocent and an unwilling participant in all Sir Buckley's crimes. Whatever he forced you to do – it is clear you did it under duress and in fear of your life. If this is so I will recommend to the law courts a fair trial. You have two options, Lundy – make the right choice, or the wrong one. If you do as I suggest you will survive. But my death, or the massacre of that girl, or the torture of any others imprisoned in these walls will result in your certain execution. Do as I have asked – send word to the village – and help will come. There is still time."

A certain softening of his resolve fluttered across his cheeks like a summer's breeze, and our pupils locked together in deepest scrutiny. For a full half minute he penetrated my gaze, and beneath that coal-black beard his unctuous tanned skin hid perfectly the spectrum of his thoughts or feelings. Was that a glimmer of humanity in his eyes, as though my appeal had somehow reached him? I could not be sure. I teetered on the point of speaking. But as though it were only a moment of brief weakness he shook his head and scowled at me.

"Pah!" he grumbled, and without a further

utterance he sailed out of the chamber, and slung the door fast with a deafening bang.

"Lundy!" I called. "Come back! Don't be a damned fool. It is your only chance! LUNDY!"

The bolts rattled in their hasps, the key was turned, and his boots echoed up the passage. I bit my lip in exasperation and moaned in perfect despair. I had squandered the one opportunity to escape this nightmare and now must wait for swift vengeance from Lundy's betrayal. He would no doubt quickly tell my tale to his master, who would prepare a special cruelty in my honour. I collapsed on the floor in doleful rage. A ravenous hunger gripped me and I set to devouring the meagre crusts that had been left below, and slaked my thirst with the foul liquid from the wooden vessel. Exhaustion had clearly dimmed my wits, because a minute later a heavy lethargy seized me, and suspecting that my food had been drugged, I slouched to the ground, in a torpid daze.

"Why won't she do?"

"Because she's as plain as a millstone! That's why! And Sir Jack wants a special kind of strumpet for the ceremony. We will prepare that pretty tramp from the tavern – a tasty morsel if ever there was one. When we have finished with this scum – go and get her ready. And leave her unspoilt too! They are his orders."

I was vaguely aware of being dragged by strong shoulders through a maze of tunnels, while these phantom-like voices seeped in and out of my conscious thoughts. Brutal hands hauled me up, and clasped me in irons once again, my head dizzy with nausea.

"Wake him up!"

A pitcher of ice-cold water was hurled in my face, and a stinging slap across my jaw roused me from my slumber. With my limbs outstretched I found myself once more manacled and chained to a beam above, and stripped to the waist. Some form of stimulants were put to my nostrils and I opened my eyes. I was in a vast square structure much taller than the banqueting hall, with huge oaken beams stretching upwards in interlocking buttresses to the roof. An arched stained-glass window of Romanesque design rose high on the back wall, a full thirty feet above floor level. The dusky glow of orange and crimson hues danced fitfully through the panes of glass, where flames from outside were reflected through their apertures. The shape and proportions of this chamber confirmed to me that I was in the central tower of Montpelier Hall, which I had hitherto not entered.

Standing before me in the middle of the floor, on a three-tiered wooden dais, was Buckley, his arms outstretched across an altar, a scarlet robe flowing from his shoulders. Around his head and neck he wore a peculiar hood of stoat and polecat skins stitched together, with the brown-and-white furs dangling like a cowl across his chest. On each side of him, one to the left, and one to the right, were two similar figures, equally draped in vivid carmine, their faces masked, wearing the same feline fur skins. At the base of the platform and forming a wide circle, stood at least twenty other figures, all clothed in scarlet cloaks, each beating out rhythms from their spirit drums, and chanting a form of incantation. Weaving in and out amongst them, and waving their arms in some repellent song, danced the same naked deviants that had seduced me earlier. Their oiled bodies slithered and gyrated, while the whites of their eyes suggested they were captive in some strange trance. Not far from me stood the execrable Kearney brothers, both muted and awaiting their orders.

At the front of the stage, and equidistant to the altar, reposed two large iron braziers, with molten flames licking brightly from their bases. A third brazier illuminated the back of the platform. Suspended from a beam in the vault, and dominating the space above this podium, hung an enormous tasselled red banner, displaying the bold black outline of an inverted pentagram. Inside its circle shone the five corners of a star, with two points raised upwards to the heavens. Embroidered in the centre sat the black symbol of a goat's head. Similar flags hanging from poles ran along the left and right sides of the tower.

I marvelled at the perspicacity of Fr. Moynihan's deductions, but even he could not have foreseen the level of complicit evil before my eyes. Here indeed was the full power of the Hellfire Club, not the vestige of a mad imagination, or the chatterings of an idle class – but a deadly reality with a Satanic purpose. I was to be its next and cherished victim.

Throwing forth both arms Buckley raised above his head a formidable blackthorn staff, twisted and gnarled from age. The wind outside moaned against the casements, as he rolled his eyes upwards.

"Oh Master, great Baphomet of the ancient realm! High God of all witches and Keeper of the secret fire! The Lord of all darkness! Hear US your faithful children who summon you to our bosoms. Long did Odin serve you, in the days of old – was it not he who gave up his blood by impaling himself on his own spear for nine days and nine nights? A deity worthy of your remembrance! And Uller! The God of Winter – with his bride Ran, the goddess of ocean storms! Great was their power to uphold your teachings as they strove to bring forth your kingdom. Aided as they were by that sorceress of the elements – Holde – the triple goddess of birth, life and death. We celebrate such great achievements and continue their mighty work. Command US your servants who beseech you to accept our humble sacrifice. Come amongst us, oh Master – and take what form you will. Your work will be our nourishment and reward."

As if in answer to his commands a violent gust outside beset the tower, rattling through the rafters and across the rooftop. Its suddenness had a startling effect upon my nerves. Then laying down the staff, Buckley produced a sword of finest antiquity, which he kissed upon the blade, holding it upright before his gathered brethren.

"Grant us our desire, mighty Baphomet, and take us through the gates of death, so that we, like you, can be reborn as perfected beings. Give us everlasting sustenance and accept our offering."

He laid the blade across the altar and grasped in both hands the horned skull of a goat's head. It had been carved somehow into a drinking vessel, to which he added a concoction of ingredients that I could not make out. Whispering some uncanny charm, he proceeded to raise it to his lips, and swallowed a mouthful of the strange mixture. Descending from the dais he held the dreadful chalice in his hands and approached me.

"Begin the initiation," he ordered.

Chanting their loud idolatrous refrains the cloaked assembly faced me, as Mick Kearney seized my left wrist. I closed my hand and resisted instinctively, but the thug almost broke my fingers as he prised them open. Swift as an arrow one of the robed congregation held up a tiny oval object in their gloved hand so that everyone present had a perfect view. It was a rune – with the same deathly symbol that I seen before, only now it was to become my sentence of execution. I writhed in fury as the egg-shaped object was placed firmly in my palm, the side that contained the etched marking touching my skin. Kearney spat on me as he crushed my fingers successfully into a closed fist.

"HE IS ONE OF US!" roared Buckley with supreme satisfaction. "Has he not accepted it into his own hand? And for that he will pay the ultimate price. Come, brothers! Samhain is almost upon us, and we have much yet to do. All must be prepared to make the ceremony perfect. Make haste to your appointed tasks. Keep our friend here alive and his mind lucid – I want him conscious when it happens."

"Just like a hare caught in a snare!" mocked Kearney triumphantly.

In solemn procession they filed out in single row, one after the other, following in the tracks of their master, as he departed the tower through a carved ebony door. The bacchanalian dancers, the masked draped figures, with the sickening rhythm of their drums – all these passed in stately fashion, until no one and nothing remained but my wretched self and the hissing coals of the burning braziers.

XVI

LUNDY'S MOMENT

An avalanche of misery overwhelmed me as silence fell on my surroundings. Caught up in a whirlpool of emotion I felt waves of vying passions breaking across my heart, before cascading backwards onto gentler shores. But at times my mind resembled a cauldron of burning oil, with hateful impulses bubbling to the surface. I tried to fight these tendencies, grinding my teeth and biting on my tongue, but I was no longer the pillar of stolid stability that I had prided myself on. A lethal combination of fear and anger was brewing in my thoughts and I felt its debilitating influence upon my resolve. I was going to die, and it would be soon. I MUST BE STRONG! I MUST!

More than any physical exhaustion emotional stress can drain us of our energies, and thus I swooned into an uneasy half-sleep. Dark were my visions as I fretted and shook, passing in and out of a tormented state. But it could not have lasted long, as I found myself once more awake – still shackled, and surveying the interior of the empty tower. Nothing could be heard except the crackling of the braziers which threw long shadows across the platform and walls. I was alone.

Like a shaft of light I now remembered those invisible voices that had spoken of a girl! Great GOD! It was

Cathy, surely, that they referred to? I surmised that it must have been my captors who had talked of her in my presence, they thinking me still unconscious. So Buckley had her somewhere in this fortress – and she was still alive. Yes! SHE MUST BE STILL ALIVE! This gave me the faintest of hopes.

By a stroke of luck, I noticed that on one wall of the tower there hung a large gold-framed mirror, dirty with age, which reflected a view of what could be seen through the window behind me. It was only a partial vista, but enough for me to gauge what was going on outside. It was still night time, and distorted though the image was, I could make out a good deal of activity – indistinct bodies flitting to and fro, some frenetically, and a massive bonfire as yet unlit. Further off I could see other piles already ablaze. My blood froze as I realized that one of these was likely to be my own funeral pyre.

Either because my senses had become keener through terror, or because the commotion outside had grown louder, my morbidity was heightened by several sounds which drew my attention. Loud screams and a chorus of shouting pierced my ears. It was a horrible noise of undiluted panic. Through the reflection of the antique glass I saw dozens of figures running in erratic fashion, some it seemed grappling with others as though in violent conflict. Precisely what they were doing I could not distinguish, but even in the dark a bright red colour shone from their garments as they gesticulated. I felt certain that the club members had already begun their planned bloodbath and that what I was witnessing was their subjugation of other victims.

While straining my eyes thus, a sudden blast shook the air outside causing me to jump. It was a sound I had heard before, but my senses were so overwrought as not to identify it immediately. There it was again – a second deafening boom, and a deep cracking, like a tree ripped asunder by a bolt of lightening! A third and a fourth followed in quick succession, until the whole hill vibrated to a clamorous din of loud explosions. Of course – I knew it now. It was gunfire!

At the same moment the heavy tread of running boots could be heard ascending the steps to the black door of the tower. Laboured panting and raised voices pounded up the stairway. So – they had come to sacrifice me at last and I must face my Maker in the next world. I could barely breathe such was my anguish – but I would fight them to the last, with tooth and fist. The huge portal was flung open with powerful energy, its terrific weight smashing against the masonry. There stood Buckley, dishevelled, perspiring, his shirt slightly torn, with a dagger drawn, staring at me with bile and vengeance. His cobalt eye flashed brilliantly, as he raised an arm to take aim at me.

But from behind him and through the open threshold, a muscular form appeared, catapulting itself like a human canon ball at the tall aristocrat. Catching him off balance the figure ploughed his shoulders into Buckley's back and sent him hurtling across the flagstones, dislodging the blade from his grasp. There in the doorway stood a stocky build bristling under a black-robed tunic, and I gasped in wonder as my misty eyes cleared to recognise Fr. Moynihan. I could scarce believe it – but there he was.

His face was florid with exertion and his eyes darted in my direction to see my predicament. No more than fractions of a second now divided his life from death, and mine also. While he had thrown a glance at me, the master of Montpelier had already scrambled along the ground and grasped once more the knife. The cleric anticipated this, and grabbing a chair from the floor, he held it up in the form of a shield. Buckley had recovered his poise and hissed at his adversary.

"Came back, did you, hooded dog? My father should have finished you off when he had a chance – filthy meddler. He flogged you once but I will make sure that you never interfere again. I will skewer you for pig feed! TRAITOROUS SCUM!"

"Give yourself up, Sir Jack!" pleaded the Corkman. "You were not always so – you were once a noble lad. We are all brought into this world unblemished – and some of us can still choose how we leave it. Turn back to the light!"

Using trim precision Buckley hurled the weapon with colossal violence at the priest's head. It glanced the side of the chair and skimmed past the monk's habit, missing its target. Any benevolence that was in the cleric's heart now evaporated, his eyes narrowing into two dark slits. Moving like a ferret the man with the cobalt eye clambered up the dais in an attempt to retrieve the ceremonial sword he had left on the altar. The Benedictine pounded after him with bold strides and in a blink was atop the platform, still holding the chair. My heart pulsated as I realised that the slightest error on the monk's behalf would result in his slaughter and my swift dispatch. I began to pull at the chains like a wild animal, desperate to free myself. What good were my arms now that I could not use them to assist the brave cleric? My skin chaffed and split as the manacles cut into my bleeding wrists.

Lunging for the hilt Buckley dived to seize it; but Fr. Moynihan brought the chair down fiercely across his arms, pinning him to the altar, then flung the sword from the top of the podium, where it clattered halfway across the flagstones – well out of reach. Landing his foot on the monk's shin the grim nobleman kicked backwards, momentarily repulsing his attacker. Both men staggered to their feet, and then began a titanic struggle between the two combatants.

Buckley struck first, thrusting his bony fingers at his opponent's face, where he crushed his nails into the priest's cheekbones. His height was a distinct advantage, as he was able to splay the robed figure flat across the altar, then proceeded to tear at his face. Gouts of blood sprang forth, and in an agony of pain the Corkman let out a bellow and bit down hard on the claw-like fingers. Buckley shrieked as he released his grip, and with herculean strength the priest raised the reprobate with both his arms, kneeing him in the groin, and then propelling him like a missile across the raised stage. A tremendous crash brought down one of the braziers as Buckley fell headlong into its path. The molten contents spewed like lava down the wooden tiers, and across the floor. One of the sparks lodged in the tassels of the Pentagram, and a thin line of flame licked sideways up the red banner. In seconds it was engulfed, as the yellow tongues leapt upwards towards the ceiling.

This commotion had distracted me to the point that I had failed to detect another person racing towards me. My first awareness of this was strong hands pulling at my fettered feet. I dropped my eyes and was amazed to see – Lundy. There he was, working zealously to free me from my bonds. Angels can take different shapes and forms, so the good book tells us, and this was a vision I could never have imagined. He recognised the shock and joy that overcame me, and seeing me flabbergasted, he spoke with assurance from his kneeling position.

"I did as yer asked, Misstuur Parsons. Der's no time ter talk – yer must git out of here at once afor de Mastuur runs ye through. Hold still while I find dat key."

He cursed and spat as he tried different keys upon the padlock, dropping the bunch several times in frustration. Sweat poured down my brow as each moment seemed an eternity. Up on the dais Buckley had found his feet, and launching himself once more, he landed a knotted fist across the monk's jawline, and punched him in the ribs with his other hand. The pair of them grappled viciously, twisting and turning across the surface of the altar, each raining blows on the other's body. I could barely watch as Buckley gained the advantage – clasping the priest's throat as he tried to strangle him to death. Through the corner of his eye Fr. Moynihan spotted a goblet of mead, as yet not toppled, and seizing it, he flung the liquid contents into Buckley's face, blinding him briefly. It worked.

With both legs raised the Benedictine kicked his attacker on the chest, and catapulted him towards another brazier. This time the scarlet cloak brushed too close to the coals and caught fire. A stunned Buckley gasped helplessly as the flames took a grip of his cape and travelled up the garment.

"Got it!" exclaimed the dwarf, as the padlock fell with a crack on the slabs, and he wrenched the coil of chains through the shackles that held me. In moments I was free. Although weakened I sprinted to the podium, with Lundy fast behind me. The fire had spread rapidly at the rear of the stand, leaping from table to chair, from banner to flag, up tapestries, and along the rafters of the ceiling. Even as I lunged to pull Fr. Moynihan away from the danger the searing heat of the combustion almost held me back.

"Get out, Daniel! Quick!" he cried, "The roof could go at any moment!"

Turning both at the same time, we watched, aghast, as a shrieking Buckley, smothered in flames, came running towards us. But he never got far – because Lundy, springing at his master's body, with dagger drawn, locked his powerful thighs around Buckley's waist, clutching him tightly as a spider crushes a fly caught in its web. Seizing the grey mane of locks with one hand, he proceeded to knife the aristocrat in a frenzied attack. I tried to separate them, but the intensity of the blaze repelled me. Again and again he stabbed, plunging the weapon into the seared flesh of his master. Only once did the nobleman wrestle the blade away from the dwarf, inflicting a wound to his side. The flames singed Lundy's hair and fingers until the pain forced him to release his grip of death.

He fell to the ground where the monk threw his cloak over him to smother the tongues of fire. I stretched out my arm to save Buckley, but he staggered backwards, his whole frame now a giant torch – and with cries that were scarcely human he plunged head first through the hissing cinders of the raging platform. He was done for. Throwing the dwarf's arms around our shoulders, we ran for our lives down the burning scaffold and through the ebony door. Thick plumes of smoke choked the stairway and made it hard to see where we were going. Descending several flights of steps we could hear a chaotic mixture of gunshots, voices, and doors banging. Several red shadows of indistinct figures barred our way, and peering through the dingy light I was ecstatic with relief to see Saunders and several of his redcoats materialise before us.

"Mr. Parsons, Sir! Thank God you are alive. We searched everywhere for you and feared the worst."

"God bless you, Saunders!" I rejoiced. "I had given up all hope. But help us quickly – both these men are injured and in great need of attention. What is the situation outside? Can we get out?"

"Colonel Butler has subdued most of the hill, Sir, and overrun the main hall, but there is a strong handful of Sir Buckley's militia still holding out and returning fire on the left flank of the building. We have taken quite a few prisoners, and Corporal Wilkinson is doing a thorough search of the vaults and store houses. We can get out by way of the servants' kitchens, and that should enable us to join up with the main detachment, without risking any crossfire."

"Excellent! Hurry now – before this fire swamps us all."

Fr. Moynihan, although bloodied, was holding up well, but I was worried about Lundy's burns and his knife wound. The going was tough as we slithered down several smoke-filled passageways, and fearing that we might still meet some resistance we kept our eyes and ears sharp. But although we encountered several of the servants, they were all subdued, fearful, and shaking. Word of the fire had spread amongst them and every soul was desperate to get out. The dissolute members of the club were not to be seen and Saunders confirmed that many had fled into the surrounding woods while others had been captured by the infantry.

Finding our way into the cook's quarters we collided with the old manservant Ben, who some days before had guided us into the banqueting hall. I insisted that he accompany us and that he bring clean cloths and a basin of water for Lundy. His eyes bristled with a strange mixture of disgust and agitation. But Saunders urged him forward, and within moments we all collapsed onto the cobblestones of the outer yard, exhausted, panting, and grateful to be alive. Leaning Lundy up against a horse's trough, both I and Fr. Moynihan supported the dwarf's head, bathed his forehead, and gave him some water to drink. He seized me by the arm, coughing and spluttering, and signalled his desperation to speak. He was bleeding badly.

"Lissthen, Misstuur Parsons! Dere is not much time, an' der are tings I must say. Me hour has cum and I'll not last out de nite."

"Rest now, Lundy," I assured him, "do not try to speak if you can't."

"I musth an' I will," he insisted, and squeezing me even tighter he pulled himself upwards towards my face.

"But yer musth understand dat I swear on me muduur's grave dat I niver had nuttin ter do wit dem murduurs. Nuttin! On me soul I giv yer me wurd. Do yer believe me? Hang me for Buckley's death if yer like – but nuttin else!"

"I believe you, Lundy – you have nothing to fear. Tell us what you know."

"Sir Jack told us he'd kill us if we said a wurd. Man, woman, or childer, he did not care. We were all ter keep our mouds, ears and eyes shut. When Sir Richuurd were still alive he had given me an' me family a hut ter live in – jeest near de wuds on de far side of de hill, wid a few goats. When Sir Jack took over – he said he'd burn me cabin down, an' kill me luved ones if we didn't do jeest as he pleased. He told de whole of Glenboyne dat he'd throw dem off der farms if dey stuud up agin 'im, as he was de owner of everyting. Sure wat cud we do? Den when Sir Richuurd died – dats when Jack turned ter even blacker ways."

"What was in that package at the smithys? Do you know anything about this monster that lurks abroad?"

"Ah, ha! So yer did not know wat it was!" he spluttered. "Der is NO MONSTUUR! Sir Jack wanted everyone te be afeard an' so he forced de blacksmith te make up a monstuur lookin' like de Divil himself. He said he'd murduur Tom if he didna do it. So de poor fella had to make a frame of metul, wid cogs an' wheels, an' a few pulleys, dat looked in de dark jeest like old Nick. Darn clever it were too. De parts cud be separated quickly, an' hid under bushes out iv sight. De chest an' shoulduurs were nuttin but metal bars covuured in heavy cloth. Both legs were wrapped wid fox an' goat hair an' a big horse shoe stuck on de end iv it, jeest like a hoofed foot. Dat's wat ye saw me carryin' in de package – a leg – you had damaged one iv dem when ye shot at it dat night in de wud. Sir Jack needed it to be repaired. He had several of dese dummies made and had dem hidden in different places around de village.

"De real monstuurs were de Kearney brudders. First dey wud kidnap a girl, kill her, an' dump de body where it wud it be found later. When dey placed dose runes in de hands I cannot be sure – maybe before de murduurs, or shortly after. Old Tom forged dem a big bellows dat made a fierce hissin' sound – jeest like an animal. When dey had killed someone dey oftin made dose noises straight after' de murduur – ter frighten away de locals. Den dey made de hoof marks everywhere, pressin dem into de mud, ter make it look like the Divil's mark! De yer get me?"

"I get you perfectly, Lundy – it is astonishing! Utterly astonishing! But why such an elaborate hoax? And why did he kill those girls?"

"Ben can tell yer dat. Can't yer, Ben? Tell Misstuur Parsons about Sir Richuurd's lettuur."

The aged retainer shook like a dandelion, his eyebrows shifting convulsively, and then, in a sobbing type of drawl, he began to speak.

"Aye – it's true – I was Sir Richard's valet these many years past, when Montpelier was still a Hall of charm and laughter. I can scarce remember a time when I didn't work here. But that was a good age ago, before he lost his wife, and worse, his sanity. I had a family of my own to feed and could ill afford to leave his employment. So I stayed.

"But often I had wished differently – such were the dark years that followed, and as each season passed my will to find a new life faded. It was on the night that Sir Richard was dying, three months back, that he summoned me to his bedside, his face filled with a mortal dread of not handing me something. Lundy was already there attempting to ease his passing. The master seemed racked with guilt, and grasping me by the arm, he thrust a letter into my palm, entreating that one of us should deliver it, that very night, to its intended recipient. I swore I would do so, but as his delirium increased he never told me the name of the person, nor wrote it on the letter. Some minutes after he gave it to me he expired, and I never found out that elusive name. Lundy insisted I read out the contents to him, which ran pretty much as follows:

"... My dearest blond darling – sweet beloved of the neighbourhood. Can you forgive an old fool for neglecting your young lips and gentle bosom? Those tender kisses are not forgotten, nor take it cruelly that I have sent you away these recent weeks. I was remiss to do so – and see it now. I utterly regret that ever Jack was born, and have only myself to blame for his debased upbringing. In truth he has become a dangerous ruffian and since his return from the continent my distrust in him has deepened. I even suspect that he may have plans to kill me! What comfort it would give me now, if our child could also take the name of Buckley. God willing, our little angel will soon be born – and see the blossoms of an early spring-time. But Jack must never find out, as I fear what he may do. Come now from Glenboyne – and I will wed you – do not delay... come swiftly my love..."

"The handwriting fell off here where his strength had failed. You may marvel that I can remember these words so accurately? But they had a profound effect upon me at the time, and I consigned them to my memory. I had just finished reading the letter when Sir Jack, entering suddenly from the door of an ante-chamber, strode towards me, and ripping it from out my hand, he read the parchment swiftly. Dreadful oaths issued from his lips, and waving his rapier at our throats, he said that if we ever revealed the import of this letter, he would drown us in the nearest corrie. From that day till this he kept us under fear of death, and so we said nothing."

"And without the mother's name," concluded Fr. Moynihan, "but raging at his father's rejection and determined to seek revenge on the unborn child, Sir

Jack took no chances and tried to kill them all – the blond, the young, the local, and the pregnant! Isn't this so, Ben?"

The aged attendant put his hands to his face, and great tears welled in his eyes as he recognised the full extent of this terrible and brutal truth.

XVII

A TIGHT STEELY FORMATION

A thunderous crash of falling masonry, splintered wood and shattering glass drew our attention to the tower behind us, where the collapsed roof discharged a powerful ball of ash and flames up into the starry night. Higher and higher they rose, caressed by a strengthening breeze, where stone and mortar now exploded under the intense temperatures. The inferno was spreading to the entire residence, and fearful of falling debris we moved closer to the gates of the outer courtyard. Out of sight, and at the front of the hall, we could still hear the pitched sounds of fighting, shrieking horses and fevered shouting.

Connected to the right apex of the building by a straggling wall, a large storehouse caught my eye, where a heavy metal trapdoor was flung open at its base, and several people came scrambling up from what seemed to be a subterranean staircase leading underground. One by one they emerged into the moonlight, and shaking themselves down they made with haste towards our company. Saunders seemed to recognise them and even gestured to the person in front. It was the remarkable Corporal Wilkinson with a band of redcoats carrying and supporting several stragglers. The black monk beamed with delight as he shot towards them and wrapped his powerful bulk around a frail bundle of shimmering blond curls. His great flaxen cloak offered protection from the biting wind, and tears welled in my eyes as I saw the gentle face of Cathy Maguire. God had been merciful to her, and I thanked him for the blessed relief of this deliverance.

She managed the faintest of smiles to acknowledge me, and my impulses wanted to embrace her in my arms and hold her tight – but I allowed Fr. Moynihan that great honour and satisfaction. I realised, too, after what Ben had revealed, that she could be with child, and her condition more vulnerable than ever. Several other girls followed close behind her – doubtless fresh victims of Buckley's recent abductions and planned assassinations. Even more amazing was the pale, unsteady figure of a limping Private Taylor, whom Wilkinson supported on his shoulder. He was still alive.

"God bless you, Corporal! You have done sterling work and you will be commended to the highest authorities for your bravery."

"All in the line of duty, Mr. Parsons – it's a miracle Saunders found you just in time. Sir Buckley had planned a massacre on the hilltop and we found these in his vaults ready to join you in some sick sacrifice. It seems he planned to burn you all alive, Sir. Tonight – on Halloween! He had already torched many cattle in preparation. Colonel Butler has brought two army surgeons with him, who are dealing with the wounded behind the firing line. We are not out of danger yet, Sir – the Kearney brothers and some of their ragtag fighters are still held up near the banqueting hall. Keep your heads low and follow me."

Thus aided by the infantry, the sick and wounded were supported out of the courtyard gates. Several overturned carts and wagons gave us some protection as we slipped past the outhouses onto the open grassland. Cavalry had taken up positions on the perimeter of the hill, and two rows of infantry, one kneeling, the other standing behind them, formed a perfect firing line, their muskets sparkling in a tight steely formation. The debris of burning wood, cast-off clothes, upturned carts, broken pikes and abandoned weapons littered the front of Montpelier Hall.

We reached the coach containing the two doctors and left all the wounded in their charge. Lundy seemed delirious and in a state of shock, while Cathy had swooned in the cleric's arms; he placed her gently on a cloak. The medical men got straight down to treating the wounds, while providing us with some desperately needed food and water. Saunders found a jacket for me, as I was near freezing.

But the siege was not over; and I instructed Wilkinson to follow me across the hilltop to join Colonel Butler's position. We scampered like mice across the tufted scrub, with the crackle of gunshot ringing in our ears, crawling at times on our hands and knees. The terrain directly in front of Montpelier Hall formed a sloping grassy ridge, interspersed with furze and gorse bushes. To gain the top of this elevation it was necessary to enter a shallow ditch or kind of moat, which was just deep enough for us to hide in, to avoid the threat of flying bullets. Here on this crescent the Commander had chosen to deploy his men, with the two lines of soldiers forming a solid column of cocked muskets. It was an impressive show of strength. Within moments we had reached him, and I thanked the Colonel for his excellent preparations.

"In the name of his majesty King George!" he cried, "surrender your weapons now and present yourselves to the Justices of the Peace! I warn you – this is your last chance!"

The Hall was almost completely ablaze, with the fire having spread from the tower through the banqueting parlour and along each of its extended wings. Below two of the large bay windows a band of Buckley's men were pent up against the building, hiding behind a large pile of barrels, wooden crates, and an overturned chaise.

"Don't listen to him, lads! You know what English justice means. A hundred lashes until your guts pour out of your stomach – or the hangmans' rope. We will not give them that pleasure. Death to your stinking King! DEATH TO OUR ENEMIES!"

While I could not see him I knew it was Mick Kearney's voice, and in response, his comrades sent a volley of shots whistling towards us. The inky cover of the night sky lent us great protection, as our foes could not distinguish our true position. We on the other hand could perfectly make out their silhouettes against the leaping flames, which grew ever closer to their backs.

The Colonel raised his cutlass from its brass scabbard, and held it high above his head.

"COMPANY!"

"POISE YOUR FIRELOCK!"

"FRONT ROW!"

"PRESENT!"

"FIRE!"

A resounding blast exploded from their muskets, shaking the very ground beneath us. The lethal bullets shot through the night air, shattering the crates into splinters and shredding the top of the chaise. Chips of stonework flew in all directions, the pellets ripping into the masonry. Remaining on one knee, the front row of marksmen prepared their cartridges. Behind them the second line of infantry stood upright.

"BACK ROW!

"PRESENT!"

"FIRE!"

Another powerful volley thundered from their firearms, tearing remorselessly into Buckley's hired henchmen. Several of the stacked barrels had fallen forward leaving their defences exposed, and parts of the building began to collapse about them where the fire had weakened the structure.

Without any warning a cluster of pikemen rose from the barrier and charged towards us, followed by several brutes with swords outstretched, and half a dozen men with weapons firing indiscriminately. The husky build of Mick Kearney took up the rear, a fiercesome axe brandished in his hands. Pouring up the ridge they came at us like wild boar, and I knew that their pikes would wreak havoc if we could not stop them.

"FRONT ROW!"

"PRESENT!"

"FIRE!"

A hail of bullets met them head on and wrought carnage in their numbers. Some fell dead instantly. Several rallied around Kearney's side and thrust out their pikes in a cordon. The pounding of horses' hooves cleft the air as the cavalry on the hilltop swept down towards them, their swords shining brilliantly. Like a breaking wave they crashed through the Irishmen, smashing open their circle of defence. Some dropped their pikes and ran for cover while others held their ground. A gripping skirmish now ensued as hand to hand combat replaced gunfire. Slashing for his life Kearney brought down several horses with his axe, while the pikemen skewered the sides of the fallen creatures. Colonel Butler had only moments to respond.

"COMPANY!"

"CHARGE!"

With bayonets glistening the redcoats sprinted down the slope and threw themselves into the struggle. Metal clashed, horses reared, and cries of human suffering drifted on the wind. Crushed below their steeds several of the cavalry were pinned to the ground. His teeth champing with fury Kearney raised his axe to cleave an officer through the skull, but a bayonet pierced him in the stomach and he slumped to his death. Seeing their loss his comrades showed no appetite to continue fighting, and throwing down all weapons they raised their hands in surrender. Skulking behind a barrel was a gibbering Pat Kearney, who crawling on all fours pleaded for mercy. He, along with the other ruffians, was arrested, chained, and put on horseback to be taken to Rathfarnham Castle.

Montpelier Hall was now completely ablaze, from the apex of its tower to its galleries, wings, sheds, and outhouses – all were consumed in a spectacular wall of flame. Its lurid secrets and dark purpose were now consigned to history. While it burned we made a thorough search of the hill and woods to root out those that had fled, especially the members of the infamous Club. None escaped our net.

As these operations continued I returned to the coaches where the sick and wounded were being tended. I was alarmed to find Fr. Moynihan sitting on a grass hummock, shaken, with tears welling in his eyes.

"What is it, Father?"

"Lundy is dead."

"Surely not!" I choked.

"It is so, Daniel. He was badly burnt and had sustained a fatal wound. In his struggle with his master, Sir Jack had plunged the blade deeper than we knew. When the surgeons removed Lundy's shirt they saw the dreadful loss of blood. It was too late."

I was saddened by this news, and sat in silence unable to respond.

"It was he who saved us all," declared the monk. "On the night of your abduction, he had it arranged to send a note to me, which was delivered to The Eagle Tavern by popping it through the broken pane in my bedroom window. I did not see it until I awoke the next morning. It was Lundy's brother that I had tried to save from a public flogging all those years ago, when Sir Richard broke his whip across my neck. In his letter Lundy thanked me for that great favour, and said his conscience could not allow another atrocity. He confirmed that Cathy had been abducted to the mountain lair, as had several other homeless girls, and that Buckley had plans to kill them all. He feared, too, for the safety of his own family. On the back of the page he had drawn a simple map of a forgotten bridle path that wound up the back of the hill, through the woods, to the summit of Montpelier. It had been used in years past as a quick escape from Jacobite attacks, but Sir Jack had forgotten its existence. An attack from this approach would have the element of surprise. He explained that the path led out of the woods onto the hilltop where a monolith stone stood very close to the western wall. There was a small gate here, which Lundy would unlock to allow us access to the stables.

"After I'd discovered his letter in the morning I knocked on your door, and finding you missing I raised the alarm. The gates of the tavern yard had been left open and we felt certain that Buckley's mob had captured you. Wilkinson was for an immediate assault but we remembered your orders to wait for the detachment, which duly came in the afternoon. We agreed to get ourselves into position, and then attack under cover of darkness. There were many obstacles that delayed us, not least fallen trees, and lame horses, but Lundy's map was accurate and the bridle path delivered its promise. We found the ancient stone, and when the bonfires were lit we burst through the unlocked gate. Lundy had been waiting and gave us access to the vaults and buildings."

"But why did he not tell me? All that time he kept me in suspense, when in fact he was an ally! His manner was always rough and unfriendly."

"Very true," agreed the priest, "he had a surly way about him – no mistake. But it is likely he trusted no one, and fearing you could betray him to his master under torture, he kept his mouth shut. Could you blame him?"

"No, Father – I couldn't. I see now that I misjudged him, and he was in every sense 'a steadfast Irishman, stout of heart, and brave of limb' – just like a certain Benedictine I know, who possesses similar amounts of courage and resourcefulness!"

To the monk's astonishment I held him in a close embrace, while praising him for tackling Buckley in the tower. His masculinity was not compromised as he smiled somewhat awkwardly, while graciously allowing me that rare and cherished moment. It was the first and only time that he would ever let me hug him.

We wrapped Lundy in a heavy cape, and a genuine regret stirred inside me that he had passed away. Cathy sighed gently in a quiet slumber and I was happy to leave her that way inside the comfort of the coach. Any wagons, traps, or horses that were not destroyed were impounded to transport the injured, the slain, or those captured. Amazingly, the infantry had sustained only minor injuries with no fatalities.

It was almost dawn, and the song thrush and linnets dared to sing out in the chilly spectral light. Splashes of gold, pink and russet red formed streaks along the horizon, and stole coyly across the tips of the spruce and mountain ash. But for the sombreness of the situation it would have been a glorious new day.

Our convoy through the mountains was slow and cumbersome but by late morning we reached the outskirts of Glenboyne. Passing through the turnpike gate the garrulous McIntyre upbraided us for not paying the toll charge, and swore that he would have to complain to the board of trustees. Pouting like a toad he turned quickly on his heels and slid back behind the window of the toll house, mouthing profanations against his Majesty's troops. Colonel Butler raised an eyebrow at the gatekeeper's zeal.

A rapturous reception ran screaming up the main street, when a pale but fully conscious Cathy climbed down from the coach, and men, women, young and old, with a party of squealing children – all smothered her in a blanket of hugs and kisses. What a contrast to when I first walked down that dismal thoroughfare when not a soul dared to show their faces. The dreadful spectre of terror now seemed to have vanished, as those that had hidden for months, even years, began to laugh, breathe, and find their voices. Several hundred now thronged the way, and a roar of cheering began as Cathy was placed upon willing shoulders, and paraded like a trophy towards The Eagle Tavern. A weaker lady might have swooned in the commotion, but the innkeeper's daughter beamed with radiant grace to the joy and delight of a recpetive and loving audience.

When they had reached the front of the tavern, a frantic Harry Maguire gobbled her up in his arms, howling like an infant that has found its mother. Sean too washed her with his tears, and picking her up like a tender lily, he carried her in his powerful arms, across the threshold and into the warmth cast by a glowing fire.

As I descended from the vehicle a pair of tiny fingers tugged playfully at my breeches. Looking down I saw the bonny features of little Tilly, her cheeks bursting with pride, as she handed me a sprig of purple heather.

"My mummy says to thank you, Mr. Parsons," she blushed, almost tripping herself up with embarrassment.

Not waiting for a reply she ran back to where her mother stood, burying herself amongst the folds of a pleated shawl. I raised the dainty flowers to my nostrils and felt as if the treasures of Solomon had been laid at my feet. The scent was sublime, and this simple show of gratitude moved me deeply. Her gesture must have been a signal, because one by one, in silent procession, each of the villagers filed past me, tipping a forefinger to their brows, some smiling at me, others nodding. None said a word. But I knew it was an Irish salute to an outsider who had gained their confidence, and it meant more to me than anything I had hitherto experienced in my life. I had earned their respect, and they let me know it. It was both humbling and gratifying.

An exploration of the grain house in the marketplace revealed that it was full of wheat, corn, oats and potatoes, which Buckley had stowed in dozens of cloth sacks. I ordered that it should all be confiscated, and immediately distributed this food to the needy and hungry. Wilkinson had the blacksmith arrested and extracted from him the location of the welded false monster parts. They were all found and transported that afternoon to the centre of the market square, where I arranged that they should be put on public display to allay any suspicions that such a creature had ever existed.

That evening the tavern echoed to the sound of merriment as news spread that Jack Buckley was dead. We ate and refreshed our exhausted bodies while the sick and wounded were given every attention. Despite all I had endured my chest wound had not deteriorated, and excluding the abrasion to the back of my neck, I had escaped any further injuries. I shuddered at the thought of what might have been.

A boisterous Harry Maguire clasped me in his arms as he shook me vigorously with heartfelt thanks and Fr. Moynihan was accorded a similar accolade. Uncomfortable with such effusive praise we both retired to the same alcove where I had displaced the table during the scuffle with the Kearney brothers. There we found a modicum of privacy and some moments to reflect on our experiences.

"How will I ever thank you, Father, for what you have done? Without your intervention I would surely have died in that dreadful tower. How did you know I was there?"

"We didn't boy! But Lundy knew – and he guided me up that staircase while he tried to locate the keys to your shackles. In the smoke Saunders had got separated from us, and I encountered Buckley alone on the landing. I tried to disarm him but he escaped from me, and I knew that if I followed in his wake he was sure to lead me to YOU. Nothing was going to stand in the way of his complete annihilation of his enemies, whether real or imaginary. This included you, his father, his tenants, or pregnant girls that carried his father's offspring.

"Buckley's arrogance had clearly led him to believe that he could murder those women with impunity, while hiding behind the fear induced by a false monster of his own making. He was certain that gossip about the Devil would keep even the bravest hearts at bay, including the authorities. Your arrival changed everything. When he failed to scare you or run you out of Glenboyne, he devised a plan for your abduction. It was necessary to kill you, but not before he had his wicked way. It seems his plan to burn your flesh as a heathen offering, along with Cathy, Taylor, and any other unfortunates he had captured, was abruptly ended when the redcoats swarmed the hill. His game was up, and he had but one goal left – to knife you quickly before being caught. But Lundy denied him that chance."

"So – Nan Harold, Mary O'Dwyer, and Therese Mulholland were all pregnant?"

"Nan certainly, the others possibly," replied the cleric. "And by whom, we do not know. My examination of Nan's corpse showed that her womb had been removed – torn out by some vile implement. This immediately made me suspicious of an unwanted child being an issue, and when you questioned the pleasurable Dr. Hannon I suspected that he, too, might have discovered this when he examined all three of their bodies. He pretended to know nothing in case his disclosure to us might reach the killer's ears and invoke punishment. To reveal that they were pregnant might also have caused great scandal in Glenboyne, and outrage from their grieving parents. Hence his silence. I'm afraid the surgeon is guilty of no crime though – only cowardice."

"And Cathy? Is she with child too?"

"Mercifully, no. Sir Jack's hatred on reading his father's letter extended to any blond girl, young and beautiful, and local to the parish, and Cathy unluckily fitted this description. Mick Kearney clearly had his own designs on her anyway, and used his master's obsession to snatch her as a scapegoat."

"But why did Buckley have Geoffrey Harold killed?"

"He did not mean to, Daniel. He was simply in the wrong place at the wrong time. Sir Jack only wanted to take his daughter – but had to dispose of the father when he was found to be with her in the chaise. Remember, he was a witness to abduction and had to be killed. The Kearney brothers had grown careless, failing to dispatch him before we arrived. Private Taylor was an unfortunate intruder too – to be removed from the scene, lest he reveal what he had spotted behind the treetops."

"Is it then your opinion that Buckley believed in this Satanism?"

"I must admit that I am still unsure as to whether Sir Jack was a believer in the black arts. He may have been, and undoubtedly his induction by Sir Richard at a young age would account for the depth of his involvement. However, on balance I feel he used their rituals as an outlet for his own twisted debauchery. It was when he read his father's letter that his mind became further unhinged, driving him to recklessness and excessive cruelty. The club, the runes, the invented creature – they were all excuses to find that one pregnancy and have it obliterated, along with the mother."

"I wonder who she was, Father?" I ventured.

"That we may never find out," he replied, and clasping the bone crucifix around his neck, he closed his eyes, and said a silent prayer.

Our last morning in Glenboyne brought forth a mild and balmy day with the Wicklow Mountains basking in a spectacular clear blue sky. Harkin had seen fit to polish the coach and had brought it around to the front of the inn for my own personal inspection. Loading our portmanteaus with a good deal of zeal, he sat atop the vehicle awaiting my instructions. Fr. Moynihan was saying his farewells, slapping the innkeeper across the back – his deep-barrelled laughter vibrating through the air. Bending forward he tenderly kissed the outstretched fingers of a delicate hand that I knew and liked so well. In every life there are a few departures that cut us to the quick and etch their memories on the fabric of our souls. This was such a moment.

Wrapped in a woollen shawl and resplendent in the early morning light Cathy came forward and curtsied to me. I could see she was tearful and I wished to spare her any unnecessary blushes. Raising her head she placed a single sweet kiss on my burning cheeks, as I looked transfixed into the depths of those huge green eyes.

"Thank you forever, Mr. Parsons. We shall never forget you."
"And I shall never forget you, Cathy. You have a good

man there in Sean. Stick with him, and you will both do well by each other. Fealty and love are rare qualities on this earth – and when you find them, never let go."

I saluted her father, while assisting the black monk into the cosy interior of the polished transport. Rapping on the rooftop I shouted to Harkin to engage the horses, and with a rattle and a groan the axles shuddered, as the worthy mares moved forward onto the high street. Through the sash I waved goodbye and realised that I might never behold that graceful form again. It was her smile that I shall always recall, imbued with love, solace, and tender decency. Brighter than a daisy she continued to beam at me, until she, the tavern and the smoking cottages, all faded from my view.

Our journey back to Dublin was unremarkable, and despite our recent memories the passage through Kelly's Gorge was both pleasant and enchanting in its natural beauty. However, I must confess it was difficult not to shiver when we passed through the shadows of that lonely hollow, which even at midday possessed an unwholesome and foreboding atmosphere. Traversing the base of the Giant's Grave we found that the mudslides had been cleared, and the road was tolerably free of fallen branches and woodland debris.

It was late afternoon when we reached the changing house at Butterfield, and with fresh steeds we made steady progress to the city walls. By eventide we had found the kerbstones of a busy Thomas Street. The hallowed steeple of the Abbey of St. John proclaimed its presence, and rapping at the coach door the Benedictine made plain his intention to alight at this spot. There was a wistful grin upon his cheeky face, with the air of a man back on his own turf. Dismounting onto the pavement he cocked an eye at me, while chirping,

"You know, boy! – you are not a bad one for an English fella."

"And you are not bad for a Corkman, Father!" I cast back, with a laugh.

He winked one hazel eye at me, and with that marvellous force of energy which defined his person – he strode breezily into the shadows of an alleyway – and was gone. It was typical of his character that he did not feel obliged to say goodbye, and I smiled at the sheer impudence of his departure. But something in me sank, as I knew that I would miss this man in the many years yet to come.

In the weeks that followed it came out in the trials that the Kearney brothers were guilty of murder, kidnap and torture, but that the eldest sibling had performed all of the atrocities. Pat Kearney was sentenced to ten years of penal servitude, and other members of Buckley's militia were given similar sentences. To the scandal of Dublin society, several members of Buckley's Hellfire Club were identified as noted aristocrats, landed gentry, and even some members of the Irish House of Commons. All were duly punished. Lundy was exonerated, buried with dignity, and given a full pardon. Tom Farrell, the blacksmith, spent a week in the stocks, but was not served with any further punishment on the grounds that Buckley had threatened him with murder, as had been all the servants of Montpelier Hall.

Most importantly of all, Fr. Moynihan was given a full and special permit to practice his faith, and was registered at Dublin Castle as a Benedictine priest. I learned some years later of his reputation in Dublin as a man of great charity, working with the homeless, the poor, and the downtrodden. He was loved and venerated by all that knew him, and his laughter became the stuff of legend.

For my part I returned to Cheshire at the end of my service in Dublin, a wiser, more rounded, and stoical individual. I was lucky by all accounts when I married the most wondrous of wives, and we settled down into a life of steady rhythms, hard work, and a table of plenty. God granted us two beautiful daughters – Tilly and Cathy – who I made sure would earn the right to uphold those names, for each and every day of their blessed lives. And this they most surely did.

THE END.

ABOUT THE HELLFIRE CLUB

Photo by Jonathan Barry

As I have located several scenes of my story at The Hellfire Club in the Dublin Mountains, I thought a few words about this place could be helpful to the reader. This is a real building which still exists today. It was built in 1725 as a hunting lodge, by a rich and influential Irish aristocrat called William Conolly, who was Speaker of the then Irish House of Commons.

At some point this lodge was rented to the infamous Hellfire Club, which was founded by Richard Parsons, the 1st Earl of Rosse, in 1735. Legend has it that this club consisted mainly of rich Irish protestant aristocrats, who indulged themselves in gaming, vice, debauchery, and Satanic worship. I saw it as an ideal setting for a purely fictional Gothic yarn. Today the building and surrounding woods are open to the public.

Jonathan Barry

ACKNOWLEDGEMENTS

A big thanks to all the team at POD Digital in Mountjoy Square, Dublin, for all their hard work in the production of this book, including Evan Kavanagh, Joanne Power, and especially to Gary Power for his excellent design of the front cover and jacket, and Kervin Arias for his great work on the textual body layout.

My gratitude also to Albert Power for his thorough editing, proof reading, and textual suggestions. For their insightful eye and helpful feedback I am grateful to Gary Egan, and Maolsheachlann O'Ceallaigh. Over the years (when completing the novel seemed daunting) the constant encouragement of Jonathan Notley, John Keenan, Colm Rath, Arnaldo Cesnik, and Diane Wohl, all helped get me to the finishing line.

Thanks also to Caolan Maher, Paul Anthony Murray, Paul Sheridan, Stephen McMullin, Dr. Rory O'Donnell, Tom McCaughren, Beatriz and Fabio Torres, Laura Carpenter, Francis Barry, and Joshua Bell. Likewise, a special thanks to Paul McGrath, Mary-Brigid Turner, Kate Murphy, and Stephen Devlin of Hodges Figgis Bookstore, and Ronan McGreevy of the Irish Times.

ABOUT THE AUTHOR

Photo by Jonathan Barry

Jonathan Barry is an internationally renowned Irish artist and book illustrator whose paintings have sold at *Sotheby's* famous auction house on New Bond Street in London. He has illustrated over seventy books, and his paintings have appeared in *The Wall Street Journal* and *The London Times*. On television his illustrations have featured in the British soaps *EastEnders* and *Coronation Street*.

Some of the books he has illustrated include: *Dracula, Frankenstein, The Hound of the Baskervilles, Peter Pan, Cinderella, Sleeping Beauty,* and *Wuthering Heights*. He is a passionate exponent of the Gothic horror genre, and since 1999 has run a Gothic Literary Book Club in Dublin, where he lives.

This is his first novel, which has received great acclaim.

Jonathan welcomes feedback. Email him at: jonathanbarrypainter@gmail.com